Return
of the Kid

**Center Point
Large Print**

Also by Wayne D. Overholser and available from Center Point Large Print:

The Long Trail North
Tomahawk
The Dry Gulcher

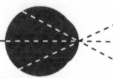

**This Large Print Book carries the
Seal of Approval of N.A.V.H.**

Return of the Kid

Wayne D. Overholser

CENTER POINT LARGE PRINT
THORNDIKE, MAINE

This Center Point Large Print edition is published
in the year 2011 by arrangement with
Golden West Literary Agency.

The text of this Large Print edition is unabridged.
In other aspects, this book may
vary from the original edition.
Printed in the United States of America.
Set in 16-point Times New Roman type.

ISBN: 978-1-61173-213-9

Library of Congress Cataloging-in-Publication Data

Overholser, Wayne D., 1906–1996.
Return of the kid / Wayne D. Overholser. — Center Point
large print ed.
p. cm.
ISBN 978-1-61173-213-9 (library binding : alk. paper)
1. Large type books. I. Title.
PS3529.V33R47 2011
813′.54—dc23

2011023028

Return of the Kid

CHAPTER I

The night that Jim Dunn returned to Cairo was a black one. The narrow gauge train, westbound for Salt Lake City, stopped only long enough to drop off a mail sack and take one on. Jim stepped down on the dark side of the track away from the depot, his badly scuffed cowhide valise in his hand, and immediately the train rolled on with a great racket of the bell and a jerking and banging of cars.

For a moment he stood beside the track, completely swallowed by darkness, the only lights those of the depot and a few places along Main Street that were still open. He shivered, not because of the October wind that rushed down from the high San Juans to the south, but from the pressing sense of danger that pricked his spine like the stab of a sharp-pointed icicle.

He had never been afraid of anything he could face, that he could actually grapple with. He had been thinking about it all the way up from Raton, but it had been sterile thinking. He had nothing to go on except Judge Riddle's note warning him to stay out of the light when he got off the train at Cairo. He would have dismissed it at once if he hadn't known the Judge too well to take a warning from him lightly.

Nothing seemed out of the way, no sound, no movement, and he decided to hell with it. If there was anything wrong, the sooner he got it into the open, the better. Picking up his valise, he strode along the track, then crossed to the other side, the cinders crunching under his boots.

As he passed the depot, he was momentarily caught in the pool of light that fell through the windows and open door. He walked fast, right hand brushing gun butt, the familiar prickle running down his spine again. Half a dozen loungers leaned against the depot wall, staring at him curiously. Jim glanced at them, thinking how typical this was. The only excitement Cairo had to offer at ten o'clock on a weekday night was the arrival and departure of the westbound train.

The men were all strangers except the town drunk, Monte Smith. Jim said, "Howdy, Monte," and walked on, amused by the way Smith's mouth fell open when recognition came to his whiskey-embalmed brain. Glancing back, Jim saw Smith whirl and plunge into the depot as if he had somewhere to go in a hurry.

For a moment the feeling of danger had left him. Everything had been in order. Time after time he had stood with his back against the depot wall and watched the train come in and leave simply because he had nothing better to do. This night was like any other night before he had left three years ago, up to the moment Monte Smith had rushed headlong into the depot. Now the instinctive alarm was set off in him again, for Smith was a man who never hurried at anything.

Jim was swallowed again by darkness. Once more the prickle died as he angled across a vacant lot to First Street and turned east along it. He had too much to think about to waste time on the danger Judge Riddle had dreamed up. The truth was he feared the moment when he must face his father far more than he feared a bullet out of the darkness. He was almost as much afraid to face Judge Riddle.

Jim had not let anyone know he was coming back. Probably Riddle would be in bed at this hour. So would his daughter Ginny. In spite of the three years that had passed, in spite of all that had happened during those years, he still felt that warm sense of anticipation that he used to feel when he came to call on Ginny, slim and blonde with eager blue eyes, the kind of girl who did not belong in the mummified life that was lived in Cairo any more than he did.

Another memory always followed the mental picture of Ginny, one that slowed his galloping heart down to a walk, that of old Judge Riddle standing in the doorway with a shotgun in his hands, bellowing indignantly, "Get out of here, Jim. If you weren't Sherm Dunn's boy, I'd blow your head off."

He had been drinking, but not enough to have

the memory of that evening blotted out of his mind. He rode off, convinced he had lost Ginny and knowing he deserved to lose her. He was young, barely twenty and Ginny not yet eighteen, but he was old enough to be certain he was in love, and more than old enough to know he should never have called on Ginny after he'd visited Rafferty's saloon.

Now, reaching the Riddle house, he paused, one hand on the gate, his eyes on the sprawling old mansion with its mansard roof, and he could not help wondering, as he had wondered for the last week, how big a fool he was to come back because Riddle had sent for him. A man had found him in Raton and handed him a sealed envelope. Inside was a sheet of paper with the two lines written in the Judge's fine, Spencerian hand: "Come home, Jim, we need you. Take a night train and be sure you stay out of the light when you get off." It was signed Judge Benjamin Riddle.

Slowly Jim opened the gate, hearing the dismal squeal of the hinges, and walked slowly up the path that bisected the big lawn. The night was so dark that he could not see more than one step ahead of him, but he had been along this path, up the steps, and across the wide porch dozens of times, and now it seemed he had been gone for three days instead of as many years, so familiar was all of this.

He set his valise down and felt along the edge of

the door until he found the bell pull; he gave it a yank and heard the metallic jangle deep inside the big house. No, he wasn't a fool, he thought. He had to see Ginny, find out if she was married, and if not, whether the old spark was still alive.

Too, there was his father from whom he had parted in anger. He had to make up, somehow, no matter how much pride he must swallow. The Box D that had been his home as long as he could remember. Maggie O'Boyle who had kept house for Sherm Dunn ever since Jim's mother had died. Sugar Sanders, the cook. Alec Torrin, the old cowhand who had taught Jim everything he knew about horses and guns and ropes. No, he wasn't a fool at all. He had a great deal to come back for, he told himself as he yanked the bell pull again. He had simply needed Judge Riddle's cryptic message to force him to a decision.

Apparently there was no light in the house. At least he could not see one through the frosted glass of the front door. Once more he jerked the bell pull, wondering if both the Judge and Ginny were gone. Perhaps he should go to the hotel, he thought, and come back in the morning.

Still he hesitated, not wanting to do that, for he had set his mind on seeing Ginny tonight, and on finding out from the Judge what his message meant. Of all the men he had ever met, Judge Riddle was, next to his father, the last man in the world who would ask for help.

Then he saw the glimmer of lamplight as someone came down the hall. A moment later the door opened and Ginny stood there, the lamp she had been carrying now placed in a wall bracket above her head. The light was behind her, throwing her shadow across the porch. Even though he could not see her face clearly, he sensed the shocked surprise that held her rigid for a moment, then he heard her whispered, "Jim."

She rushed toward him headlong and put her arms around him and hugged him with all her young strength. She said over and over, "Jim, Jim, I didn't think you'd ever come back." Then she was kissing him, pulling his head down so that his lips could meet hers, and thus she gave him the answers to the questions that had been in his mind. She still loved him and she wasn't married.

Suddenly she pulled away from him as if remembering something she should never have forgotten in the first place. She stepped back into the house, drawing him after her and shutting the door. She looked at him closely, her face troubled. "You shouldn't have come back, Jim," she said. "I would have gone if you'd sent for me."

For the first time he could see her face clearly. There was no change except the natural one that time brings to a girl of seventeen. She was twenty, a woman with a woman's mature body. For a moment he was content to simply stand and look at her, then he realized what she had said.

"Why shouldn't I have come back?" he asked.

"Because they'll kill you." She swallowed, then she cried out, "Why didn't you write to me? You just rode away without leaving me word of any kind." She paused, and he saw bitterness darken her face, and she added resentfully, "You've treated me badly, Jim. For all I know, you're married and you've got five kids."

"Not in three years," he said. "I'm sorry, Ginny. There never was a day from the night the Judge ran me off your porch with a shotgun that I haven't loved you."

But the first flush of pleasure that came from seeing him was gone. She stood with her back against the wall, her body rigid. She said, "Three years without a post card. Did you think I was going to be an old maid just because I was hoping you'd . . . you'd . . ."

She stopped, her firm, pointed breasts rising and falling with the intensity of her breathing, her full lips that normally tipped upward in a smile now pulled tightly against her teeth. No use to apologize, he thought. No use to tell her he wasn't much for writing, that he wasn't sure what she thought of him after that night the Judge had run him off, or whether the Judge might have poisoned her against him. No use to say anything. If he stayed, he would have to start courting her all over again. If he didn't, she would be better off if she could hate him.

"What was that you said about killing me?" he asked. "Nobody on this range wants to kill me." She said nothing for a moment, and he thought again of her father's warning. Then he said, "I forgot Frank Castleman. Is he still around?"

"He's working for the Mercantile, but he's not the one I meant. This range isn't the same as when you left." She whirled and started down the hall. "Dad will want to see you. He's in the study."

Jim followed her, walking slowly, depressed by her change of mood. Yet he could not blame her. He had treated her badly. Looking at it from her viewpoint, it was natural enough for her to say he could at least have sent her a post card. But there was something he could not tell her, something he had never fully defined in his own thinking. His father had ordered him off the Box D. After he'd gone, he'd had a feeling he must prove himself by going away to places where his name meant nothing, where the Box D might have been another ten-cow spread making a poor living for its owner. But now that he was back, he wasn't sure he had proved anything in the three years he had been gone.

Ginny opened the study door, calling, "Jim's here, Dad."

He stood behind her, looking over her shoulder at Judge Riddle who was on his feet staring at him. For a long terrible moment he had to fight an impulse to run. Riddle had sent for him, Riddle had said they needed help, Riddle had warned him to stay out of the light when he got off the train. But now, his gaze locked with the old man's, Jim could find no hint of welcome in the craggy face.

"Come in, Jim," Riddle said. "Leave us alone, Ginny."

Jim forced reluctant feet to carry him into the study. Ginny hesitated, then moved back and shut the heavy oak door. Still Riddle did not move from where he stood in front of the fireplace. He was a big man, almost as tall as Jim, and in his youth had been an active one.

Riddle was over sixty now, with deep lines carved into the flesh of his face, a bristling white mustache and a mane of white hair that lifted directly above his forehead and was brushed back so it gave the appearance of a magnificent plume that waved back and forth as he tipped his head. Years ago he had buried an ax in his left knee and when the wound had healed, his leg was bent so it was a good six inches shorter than his right. To walk at all, he had to wear a heavy, built-up shoe on his left foot which added to the appearance of massive strength that to Jim had always been an inherent part of the man.

"Why did you come back, Jim?" Riddle asked.

His tone was stern, demanding, and the feeling of depression that Ginny had aroused in Jim gave way to anger. "That's a hell of a question, Judge.

15

You know the answer as well as I do. You sent for me."

A hint of a smile curled Riddle's liver-brown lips. "Yes, I did. I spent nine hundred dollars on a detective who traced you from hell to breakfast. The only information we had was that you'd killed a man in Las Vegas two years after you left here. He followed your trail down through New Mexico to El Paso where you killed a second man six months ago, then across Texas to Lamar, Colorado, and back to New Mexico where he found you in Raton. But you haven't answered my question."

Riddle had put an unfair light upon the killings, and anger stirred deeper in him. "About those men I killed," he said. "The one in Las Vegas was part of an outlaw bunch that was holding up a bank. The one in El Paso was a gambler who had been dealing crooked. When I jumped him he pulled a derringer on me. I'm not ashamed of either."

"I didn't aim to make it sound as if you should be," Riddle said. "I mentioned the incidents because they were the means by which the detective was able to trace you." He reached for his cane and took three hobbling steps toward Jim. "I'm looking at a different fellow from the brawling, gambling pup who had been spoiled by Sherm Dunn. I'm seeing a man who looks as if he might have worked for his thirty a month and beans. You're taller than you were, six feet two,

I'd say, and you'll weigh close to one hundred and eighty pounds. I'm guessing that you're handy with that hog leg you're packing. Am I right?"

Jim nodded, completely puzzled. "I don't savvy what you're getting at, Judge."

"Answer my question. Why did you come back?"

Jim's temper turned edgy again. "Damn it, you sent for me. You said you needed help. I figured I could give some."

"That's what I wanted to hear, Jim." Riddle limped forward, his hand extended. "When you left here, you wouldn't have crossed the street to help anybody, but I figured you'd come out all right." His hand gripped Jim's and then as he let it go, he added. "There's several things I've got to tell you. The first one is that I'm afraid I fetched you back to get shot."

CHAPTER II

A few minutes before Ginny had said much the same thing. Like any woman, she might have spooked at a shadow, but it took something more solid than a shadow to scare Judge Riddle. Jim said, "Make it plain, Judge."

"Sit down, boy." Riddle motioned toward a black leather chair in front of the fireplace, then hobbled to his desk and dropped into the swivel chair. "Have you heard anything that's happened here, anything at all?"

"No."

Riddle leaned back and filled his pipe, the ominous silence running on for a full minute. Jim rolled and lighted a cigarette, glancing around the room. One entire wall was composed of shelves that were filled with law books, the other three walls were of oak paneling, but nowhere was there a single picture to break the dark monotony. The huge stone fireplace, the roll-top desk, the high-piled maroon carpet: all of it combined to give an impression of massive strength, as typical of Judge Riddle as the Box D with its big ranch house and barns and corrals were typical of Sherman Dunn.

In many ways the two men were alike. They were the best of friends, they were the same age, they had come here twenty odd years ago when the Ute reservation was first opened to settlement. Together they had founded the town of Cairo, together they had started the bank. Riddle had built up his law practice, Sherm Dunn had moved out to Ouray Creek and started the Box D. Both had believed in the solid, careful way of life, and they made Cairo their kind of town. Both had lost their wives several years ago, and both had one common weakness: their children. Jim understood that now. He would not have admitted it three years ago if he had understood it.

"Funny thing," Riddle said at last. "You think you know a man when you've worked hand and glove with him for twenty some years. You think you can predict what he'll do, then he completely fools you."

Jim knew what he meant. It brought back the old, deep ache he had tried to forget, the memory of his one, violent quarrel with his father, of angry bitter words he had since regretted. Probably his father had regretted his, too.

"You said something about fetching me back to get killed," Jim said.

"I'll get at that in a minute," Riddle said. "There's another thing I've got to tell you first. I'd rather take a whipping, but the sooner you hear it, the better. Your father was killed six months ago."

Jim stared at Riddle, his first reaction one of sheer disbelief. He had never thought of death touching his father. At sixty Sherman Dunn had been able to do the work of a young man. As far as Jim knew, he had never been sick a day in his life. He had always demanded the most from the men who rode for him, but never more than he demanded from himself. To Jim he had been like the great, serrated peaks of the San Juan range to the south: they had always been there, they always would be there.

Jim tossed his cigarette stub into the fireplace. He asked, "How did it happen?" But Riddle didn't answer the question, and Jim probably would not have heard him if he had. He was stunned; he felt as if it had suddenly become night in the middle of the day. Only time could bring his life into focus with the fact that his father was gone. He had intended to come back and make up and then ride on, for he had long ago decided that the Box D would never be his home again, but the days had become weeks and the weeks months, and the possibility that his father would not be alive when he returned had never entered his head.

He was aware that his question was still unanswered, and he turned his eyes to the Judge, asking again, "How did it happen?"

"Nobody knows for sure," Riddle said. "Apparently his horse threw him when he was riding down into Elk Canyon. You know how it is, a sheer drop of two hundred feet or more, and there's some slide rock about halfway down that makes pretty touchy going. All we know is that Bud Colter, he's the Box D foreman, found him at the base of the cliff, busted all to hell. He'd been dead about twelve hours, Doc Finley figures."

"What horse was he riding?"

"Sundown."

"That's crazy." Jim got up and walked to the desk. "Judge, you know as well as I do that Sundown would never throw him. Likewise you know he wouldn't slip on that slide rock. Dad wasn't afraid of anything, but he never took crazy

20

chances, either. He was always careful on that piece of trail."

"I know," Riddle said. "But he's dead."

"This man Colter. You say he's foreman?"

Riddle nodded. "Luke Dilly pulled out a month or so after you left. I never had a chance to talk to him and Sherm wouldn't tell me whether he fired Dilly or Dilly just quit. Anyhow, he hired Colter a month or so later. That's part of what I meant a while ago when I said you think you know what a man will do, then he turns around and does something you never thought he would. Hiring Colter, I mean. He's a hard case, Jim, a real tough hand. Most of the old crew's gone. Sugar Sanders is still cooking. Lennie Nolan and Alec Torrin are there. The rest pulled out inside a year after Colter took over."

"Maggie?"

"Oh, you couldn't drive her off the Box D. She said you'd come back."

Jim swung around and walked to the fireplace. There was one more question he had to ask. He was afraid of the answer, for he thought he knew what it would be. "What about that woman?"

"Sherm married her the day after you left."

"What's she like?"

"I don't know, Jim. She's got the face of an angel, and she acts like an angel, and all the time you keep wondering if she's the devil in disguise. You'll have to go out there and see for yourself."

21

Jim wheeled to face Riddle. "The hell I will. I don't ever want to see that bitch." He turned around again and put a hand on the mantel, and once again he asked himself the old, sickening question. How could this thing have happened in the first place?

Sure, he had been young and willful, and he'd been spoiled, so there were times when he'd said things to his father he shouldn't have said. But he'd worked. If he hadn't been a good hand, Luke Dilly would have told him to stay in the house and keep books for his dad. Well, he'd done that, too, in evenings or Sundays if he didn't have too much of a hangover.

Now, thinking back over it, Jim realized there was something incongruous about a sober, stable man like Sherman Dunn having a boy who drank too much and gambled too much and got into too many fights. Sooner or later it had to come to a showdown, but the odd part was that when it did, it wasn't over Jim's drinking or fighting. It was over a woman, Ann Delaney.

Sherm Dunn met her in Pueblo. Jim hadn't heard how. She was thirty-two years old and she was pretty, or so Sherm said. When he told Jim about her, he had a strange look in his eyes, almost as if he were hypnotized. "She's wonderful, Jim," he said reverently. "I never thought it would happen to me, to fall in love again, and with a woman like Ann."

Jim wouldn't have said a word if his father had married a woman his own age. Or someone a few years younger like Maggie O'Boyle who had loved Sherm as long as she'd kept house for him. But a young woman, a fortune hunter! It was too much and they had quarreled.

The real break had come a week later, the night Judge Riddle had run Jim off the porch with a shotgun. Jim was hurt and angry, and worse, he condemned himself for stopping at Rafferty's saloon before going to see Ginny. When he got home, his father said with great pride, "Ann's here, Jim. We're going to be married in the morning. I want you to meet her tonight."

That was it. Jim could not remember exactly what he had said, or what his father had said, but he remembered well the bitterness and the violence, and the woman calling from the head of the stairs, in a clear, sweet voice, "No, Sherman, no. I don't want to come between you and Jim."

"Get out," Sherm had said then. "Get off the Box D and don't come back until you're man enough to get down on your knees and ask Ann to forgive you."

Well, he was back, but his father would not be on the Box D to judge how much of a man he was. Suddenly he was aware that Riddle had crossed the room to him and laid a hand on his shoulder. He said, "Jim, listen to me. I quarreled with Sherm about her, too, but I guess he had a right to do what he wanted. It was just that it didn't seem like Sherman, marrying a woman like her and hiring a hardcase to rod the Box D."

Jim stared at the Judge's face, hard set and made bitter by old, returning memories. Jim said, "You think she killed him, don't you? Or had Colter do it?"

"I don't know," Riddle said heavily. "There's no evidence. Maybe if you lived there on the Box D for awhile, you could find some." He dropped his hand, shaking his head at Jim. "You don't want to see her, but you've got to. The will Sherm left is a strange one. You see, he always was ashamed of himself for sending you away, but he said it was the best thing that had ever happened to you, and maybe it was. Anyhow, the will leaves everything in abeyance for one year. None of the property can be sold, and during that time neither you nor Ann can draw more than fifty dollars a month for spending money. I've been paying the bills because I'm the administrator, and I've deposited the money that Colter turned over from the sale of the herd."

"They've finished roundup?" Jim asked.

"Last week. Well, during this year, or the six months that's left of it, you must live on the Box D and run it to my satisfaction. If you do, the Box D goes to you and a cash settlement to Ann. If you don't, or if you die before the year's over, everything goes to Ann."

Jim's first impulse was a rebellious one. He wanted to say to hell with it, then a stubbornness took possession of him. The woman had no right to the ranch, she had no right to even be there. Now, looking squarely at Riddle, he knew the Judge would expect nothing very great from him.

"All right," Jim said. "I'll try. I may twist her damned neck, but I'll try."

A faint smile touched Riddle's mouth. "I know how you'll feel, living there with her. Just do the best you can. I'll ask for nothing more." He hobbled back to the desk. "Stay here with us tonight, Jim. We have plenty of room."

"No, I'll be better off at the hotel. I've got some thinking to do." He picked up his hat from the corner of Riddle's desk and twisted the brim in his hands. "Judge, the last time I saw you, you made it clear I was to stay away from Ginny. That still go?"

"Hell no. You've grown up. That's all I ever expected. Sherm and me used to talk about you and Ginny. He said Ginny wouldn't work hard enough to be a rancher's wife, and I said you hadn't settled down enough to be a rancher. But that was three years ago, I'd say we were both wrong. Well, it's up to you and Ginny. Just one thing, Jim. Be careful."

Jim hesitated, wanting to tell Riddle how he felt about Ginny, but it didn't seem to be the time or place. Six months from now would be the time, and maybe the Box D would be the place. But there was still one question that had to he asked.

"What about that help you . . ."

"It can wait until you get the feel of things," Riddle said. "I'll see you in a day or two."

"I'll look for you," Jim said, and left the study.

He did not see Ginny until he was on the porch. He heard her call, "Jim," and turning, made out her vague figure standing against the wall far from the lighted doorway.

He went to her and took her hands. He said, "I've got a job to do, Ginny. If I live, and if I get the job done, I'm going to ask you to marry me. Right now I just want you to wait six months for me. Is that too much to ask?"

"No, Jim," she said in a worried tone, "but I don't want you to go out there. I'm afraid of her. If you love me, you'll marry me now."

"I left here with forty-nine dollars in my pocket," he said. "I've got sixty-two now. Not much savings for three years' work, Ginny. Not much to support a wife on, either."

Wheeling, he strode off the porch and down the path. He wasn't sure Ginny understood. He wasn't sure she would wait for him, or that he even had the right to ask her to.

CHAPTER III

Bud Colter was a vain man. He knew it, and it bothered him not at all. He often said to Ann Dunn that everyone loved himself. The only difference between Bud Colter and other people was that he didn't deny it. Others did. You took all you could for yourself if you had a chance to take anything. If you didn't have a chance, you manufactured one. That is, if you were smart, and Bud Colter was smart, for that was exactly what he had done when he'd introduced Ann to Sherm Dunn, and then made a widow out of her.

Colter had never been a patient man, and now what little patience he did have was wearing thin, but he had to play it out for six more months. He'd invested three years of time already and he'd committed one murder, although the murder bothered him less than the time. The six months he had to wait until Ann took over all of old Sherm's property didn't seem very long when he measured it against the three years that were behind. That thought always calmed him.

On the night Jim Dunn returned to Cairo, Colter stood at the bar in Rafferty's place, an empty shot glass between the thumb and forefinger of his right hand, a half-filled bottle in front of him.

27

Ordinarily he drank very little, but he was in a sour mood tonight and the whiskey helped.

He'd known Ann for eighteen years and, by God he still couldn't make her out at times. She wasn't stupid. That much was sure. She must have guessed what had happened to old Sherm. Lately she'd been acting as if it wouldn't take much to make her talk. She didn't know anything actually, not anything she could tell in court. If she got far enough out of line, he'd tell her he'd swear she'd hired him to kill the old bat. After all, she was the one getting the property. That'd shut her up quick enough.

He poured another drink and let it stand, his eyes lifting to the back bar mirror. This was his favorite spot because he could see himself and he liked what he saw. At thirty-eight he had no trace of white in his black hair or his bushy brows. The same was true of his heavy mustache.

He was proud of this, for black was an obsession with him. He wore a black Stetson that had cost him forty dollars, a black shirt, black trousers, and a black-butted gun in a black leather holster which hung from a black belt. The only breaks in the somber monotony were the row of pearl buttons down the front of his shirt and the sterling silver belt buckle.

His one regret was the fact that his eyes were blue. The rest of his face he loved: the square chin, the heavy lips, the high cheekbones, and above all, the long, slightly hooked nose. He resembled an eagle, he decided as he lifted the glass and took his drink, an eagle with wide, muscular shoulders and a body that tapered down from that great width to small feet encased in expensive, high-heeled boots.

He'd fooled a lot of people, he told himself, including the sheriff, young Hank Watrous. He could get along without the old fools like Judge Riddle and Doc Finley as long as he had Watrous on his side. And Frank Castleman. Now there was a good tool just waiting to be used, shiny bright and honed to a fine edge. All he had to do was jerk the string.

He reached for the bottle, pleased with himself, then he realized a man was pressing against his left side, and the moment of self-adoration was gone. He smelled the fellow's breath and knew who it was before he turned his head. Monte Smith was another tool, poor, rusty metal, but one he could use. He said, "Howdy, Monte."

Smith said, "Buy me a drink, Bud."

"Go to work, Monte, if you want good liquor," Colter said. "It's a shame for fine talent like yours to be wasted."

The brown tip of Smith's tongue touched his lips, then the lips sprang back from snaggleteeth in what was meant for an ingratiating grin. "I am working, Bud. For you. I've got news. It'll cost you a drink and a silver dollar."

Colter smiled and motioned to Rafferty. "A glass for my friend Monte," he called.

Rafferty grunted something as he placed a clean glass in front of Smith. After he walked away, Smith muttered, "He's got no call to act that way. Just 'cause I owe him a little money, he don't . . ."

"Someday I'll clear that bill up for you, Monte," Colter said expansively as he poured Smith's drink. "What's the news?"

Smith took the drink in one gulp, set the glass down, and wiped his mouth with the back of a hairy hand. "A silver dollar like I told you. No greenback."

"What difference does it make? You won't keep it long."

"I like to feel it."

Colter laid a dollar on the bar and Smith slipped it into his pocket, keeping his fingers wrapped around it. He said, "Jim Dunn got in on the ten o'clock."

Colter had been expecting to hear this for weeks, but now that he did hear it, he had to struggle to mask his surprise. He said easily, "Hell man, what made you think that was worth a drink and a dollar?"

"Oughtta be worth more," Smith said, aggrieved. "He'll go right out to the Box D, won't he? I'll bet this here dollar you're fired afore tomorrow night. He liked them old hands you kicked off the ranch. I'll bet . . ."

"I'd take the bet if I didn't know you'd have that dollar spent before tomorrow night." Colter nodded. "So long, Monte."

He left the saloon, walking rapidly as soon as the bat wings flapped shut behind him and he was out of the light. He turned right at the corner, considering what Jim Dunn would do. He would probably get a room at the hotel. It was very unlikely he'd ride out to the Box D tonight, especially if he'd heard about old Sherm and knew that Ann was out there. If he hadn't heard his dad was dead, he'd hear mighty soon after he got to town.

One thing was sure. He'd want to know about the will. Any sane man would, with a fortune dangling between him and Ann Dunn. That answered the question. He would go first to Judge Riddle's place. After that? Well, it didn't matter. If Colter had it figured right, Jim Dunn wouldn't go anywhere.

Frank Castleman lived in a small house on the bank of the Uncompahgre River. The place belonged to Bill Royal who owned the Mercantile. Castleman worked for Royal, taking the use of the house as part of his pay. When Colter knocked, Castleman called, "Come in." Colter opened the door and stepped inside, wondering as he always did whether Castleman invited everyone in who knocked or if he had no other visitors.

Castleman was in his middle twenties, sandy-

31

haired, stocky of build, and possessing the greatest capacity for hatred Colter had ever found in a human being. He was sitting in front of the stove, a cup of coffee in his hand. Without looking around, he said, "Have a chair, Bud. I'll get you some coffee."

"Can't stay," Colter said. "Jim Dunn's in town. Got in on the ten o'clock. I'd better light a shuck out to the Box D and tell Mrs. Dunn. I thought you'd want to know, so I dropped by."

Castleman said, "She'll never see him." He put the empty cup on the floor beside the chair, and rose. He looked at Colter, his square, freckled face devoid of expression. "It'd be a shame for a widow not to inherit all of her husband's property, wouldn't it, Bud?"

"Why yes, I suppose . . ."

"I figured you'd think that, especially when the widow's young and as pretty as Mrs. Dunn." Castleman walked past Colter, took a Winchester down from a set of deer antlers on the wall and jacked a shell into the chamber. "Got any idea where Jim is?"

"No, but it stands to reason he'd go to see Judge Riddle first thing. He'd want to find out about the will."

Castleman nodded, his faster breathing the only sign that tension was growing in him. "Sounds reasonable, all right. How much you paying for this job, Bud?"

Colter stared at him, the sense of mastery draining out of him. For more than a year he had carefully cultivated Castleman's friendship, dropping in to talk or play cards, and all the time he had considered Castleman far below average in intelligence. He must be to live by himself and think of nothing but killing Jim Dunn.

"Now look, Frank . . ." Colter began.

"No, you look," Castleman broke in. "You're a tough boy, Bud. You let everybody know it. You put on quite a show with your black duds and your black-butted six-shooter and all, but you don't fool me a little bit. I knew old Sherm too well to think he'd get himself killed riding down into Elk Canyon. You're set up real fine if Jim never came back, but you say he is back. All right, you need him out of the way. I aim to put him out of the way, but I might as well get paid for it. How much?"

"Go to hell," Colter said, and spun toward the door.

"You go through that door before we make a deal," Castleman said, "and it'll be you I'll plug, not Jim. Turn around."

Slowly Colter made the turn. "Five hundred dollars the day they bury him."

"And another five hundred the day you marry the widow."

Colter nodded. "You made a deal," he said.

Castleman went out through the kitchen and a

moment later Colter heard the back screen slam. He left through the front, cursing as he walked in long strides to his horse that he had left on Main Street. This business with Castleman had not gone the way he had planned, largely because he had misjudged the man. Castleman had put into words what a great many people undoubtedly thought, that Bud Colter had murdered Sherman Dunn, and when the muddied waters had cleared, he'd marry Ann and have it good the rest of his life.

Well, let them think what they wanted to, he told himself savagely as he mounted. They couldn't prove anything. If Castleman shot young Dunn, it was well worth a thousand dollars. If he didn't Colter would have to figure out a way to do the job himself, something like what had happened to old Sherm in Elk Canyon. But he'd worry about that later if he had to. Right now he had one more thing to do and not much time if Jim Dunn kept on the move.

Sheriff Hank Watrous lived on the south edge of town across the bridge from Frank Castleman's place. He came to the door when Colter knocked, walking in his socks, his shirt unbuttoned, his pants held up by one red suspender, the other dangling. From the back of the house Colter could hear a sick baby crying, and from the look on the sheriff's face, Colter saw the man was in a fretful mood.

"Howdy, Hank," Colter said. "Sorry to bother

you this late, but I've got something to tell you."

"Oh, it's you, Bud. Come in." Watrous sighed and turning, placed the lamp he held on the paint-peeled stand in the middle of the room. He motioned to a chair. "Sit down."

Colter dropped into a rocking chair that was held together with baling wire. Watrous was in his early thirties, a tall, slender man with a receding hairline and deep lines in his face that added years to his appearance. His wife wasn't well, he was in debt to Doc Finley and Bill Royal at the Mercantile, and he was behind in his rent to Judge Riddle who owned the house he lived in. He'd owned a small farm on the river below town which had been taken over by the bank more than a year ago. After that, he'd run for sheriff, and to everyone's surprise, he had been elected.

Colter got out a cigar and lighted it, glancing at Watrous who sat on the edge of his chair as if waiting for his visitor to state his business and leave. The house was dirty and needed airing, it smelled of soiled baby clothes, and at the moment Colter wasn't sure whether he could make himself stay long enough to establish the alibi he was going to need or not.

"I've got something to tell you, like I said," Colter began, "but I want to ask a question first. Why does Castleman hate Jim Dunn the way he does? I came here after Jim left the country, and Castleman ain't of a mind to talk about it."

Watrous stirred impatiently, his head cocked as if listening, and it took a moment for Colter to realize that the baby was still crying. "My youngest has got the colic," Watrous said. "Don't look like my wife or me'll get much sleep tonight. I was up all last night, you know. Had to go clean back into the 'dobe hills after Orie Mann. Got into a scrap with Vic Teller over water, Orie did. Hit him with a shovel and damned near killed him."

Colter jerked his head toward the bedroom. "Why don't you call Doc for the baby?"

"I owe him too much now," Watrous said. "Anybody in my family is gonna be mighty sick afore I call the doc. He ain't never refused to come, mind you. It's just that, well, I'm trying to get out of debt and it don't look like I'll ever make it."

"You'd have made it all right if the bank hadn't closed you out," Colter said. "Must be a bunch of bastards running that bank."

"Yeah, and old Sherm Dunn was the Number One Bastard in the county when he was alive," Watrous said glumly. "Now that he's kicked the bucket, I suppose Mrs. Dunn will go on running things like Sherm done."

"No, don't figure she will," Colter said blandly. "I'm sure of just one thing. She's not grabby like Sherm was. No sir, if Mrs. Dunn ever gets a controlling interest in the bank, a lot of things will be different than they were."

"I hope so," Watrous said. "Won't do me no good, times being what they are, but there's a hell of a lot of poor devils in the valley who are in the same boat I was in before I lost my shirt."

"I asked about Frank . . ."

"Oh yeah. Well, that goes back to when Jim was here. Always brawling, Jim was, and gambling. Drinking, too. Sherm spoiled him. Gave him more money than he should have. But I will say one thing for Jim. He was a hell of a good poker player, even when he was a kid. Frank is some older'n Jim. He had a little place next to the Box D. Ran it by himself and had ever since he was seventeen when his folks died o' typhoid.

"This happened in the fall almost four years ago to the day. Frank had just shipped some cattle and he had 'bout eleven hundred dollars in his pocket. He got to playing poker with Jim and Doc Finley and two or three more. I think Bill Royal was one. They started one night and played till morning, and at one time Frank had better'n three thousand dollars in front of him. 'Bout sunup his luck turned and he started losing. By noon he was clean. Just Frank and Jim and Doc in the game by that time.

"Well, Frank got a good hand. I disremember what it was, but he stopped the game long enough to go over to the bank and mortgage his spread for all he could get. He lost the hand to Jim who was holding four aces. Wasn't long till the bank took the ranch and Sherm bought it from the bank. Of course that was what he wanted all the time. Frank figured it was a put-up job. He brung it all on himself, but you couldn't never tell him that."

Colter knew all this, but he was playing for time, listening for the shots that should have come before this. Watrous began fidgeting impatiently, now that he'd answered Colter's question in his long-winded way. It was enough to let Colter know he'd stayed out his welcome.

"Funny thing about Castleman," Colter said as he rose. "Seems like he don't want nothing out of life but to get square with Jim Dunn."

Watrous nodded. "It's been eating on him all this time. It got worse after Jim left. Frank began kicking himself for not shooting Jim . . ."

The shots came then, two cracks of a rifle, so close together they seemed to make one sustained sound. Watrous jumped up, but before he could say a word, even before the echoes of the rifle had completely died, another gun was fired.

"That last one sounded like a .45 to me," Colter said.

"What the hell's broke loose?" Watrous demanded.

"What I came in to tell you was that Jim Dunn's back in town," Colter said. "Got in on the ten o'clock . . ."

"You're a hell of a long time telling me," Watrous said angrily, and started toward his bedroom. "Wait'll I pull my boots on."

"No, I'd best get along," Colter said. "I don't want to get mixed up in it."

He left the house, hearing nothing more from Watrous, and stepping into the saddle, took the road that led south across Ruby Mesa and down into Ouray Valley that held the Box D. Now the sourness was gone, and a heady sense of satisfaction filled him at the way this had worked out.

Ann would be in bed, but he'd get her up to tell her. Six months more, and then everything would go to her: the Box D, the bank, the cash on deposit, several pieces of town property. Suddenly Bud Colter began to whistle.

CHAPTER IV

When Jim left the Riddle house, he had only one thought in mind, to reach the hotel and get a room and shut the door. He wanted to be by himself, to adjust his thinking to the shocking fact that his father was dead. He simply could not imagine the Box D without his father's domineering presence.

He made the turn into the business block, thinking how dark it was, and quiet, totally unlike other towns where he had tarried during the past three years. Cairo had been and probably still was a respectable town, a nice town intolerant of sin and violence except on Saturdays when the farmers came to shop during the day and the cowhands to raise hell by night.

This situation struck Jim as being incongruous. On Saturday Cairo was a different town than it was on the other six days of the week. The bank stayed open until eight at night, the Mercantile until ten. Judge Riddle remained in his office as long as the store was open. Rafferty hired an extra bartender and both of them were kept on the jump until after midnight. Bill Royal in the Mercantile hired two extra clerks. As far as the law was concerned, anything short of murder and horse stealing was condoned. Then, on Sunday morning, Cairo tucked its tidy skirts around its ankles and was a prim old maid for the next six days.

Jim had never given this strange hypocrisy any serious thought when he'd lived here, but he did now because he had seen so many other places that were frankly wide open all week or held the same standards on Saturday that they did on the other six days. He wondered if there was a weakness in his father's character that was somehow reflected in the town's double standard.

He decided the thought was unworthy and he put it out of his mind, but he mentally recognized another fact that had not occurred to him before. He had never fitted here because of Cairo's six-day respectability. He would have left sooner if he hadn't been Sherman Dunn's son.

Now he wondered if he could stay, if either he or the town had changed enough to permit him to make his home. . . .

Gunfire sliced at him from the darkness across the street, two rifle shots, the last cracking into the echo of the first. One was a complete miss, the second lifted his hat off his head. His action stemmed from the sheer instinct of self-preservation. Dropping his valise, he fell belly flat against the front of the Mercantile. He heard tinkling glass fall from a window, then he drew his gun and threw a shot at the place where the dry-gulcher had been standing.

Foolish, he thought, just plain, damned stupid. He lunged forward, not stopping until he was ten feet from where he had lain when he'd fired. The ambusher must have fled, for there were no more shots. If he had remained, Jim's gun flash would have given him a target he could hardly have missed with only the width of the street between them.

Jim sat up and felt around in the darkness for his hat. Sweat had broken out all over him and he began to shake. This was what Riddle had meant in his note; it was what both the Judge and Ginny had meant when they'd said he'd get killed. He found his hat and stood up. Suddenly he was both angry and scared, angry because of the method the killer had taken, and scared because there was nothing more dangerous than a coward

41

who would bushwhack a man.

He stepped back to where he had dropped his suitcase. He picked it up and holstered his gun. Rafferty's place was thirty feet ahead of him. If the killer had waited, he would have had Jim pin-pointed against the lighted windows of the saloon. Jim considered that, and found no adequate explanation unless the dry-gulcher had been swept away by panic and been unable to control himself. Or perhaps he had realized that men were in the saloon and one of them might have been hit. But such a humanitarian thought seemed out of place in a killer who shot from ambush.

He had no more time to think about it. Now that it was plain the shooting was over, men poured out of the saloon, Bill Royal in front, Rafferty behind him and puffing at every step, and half a dozen others. Royal called out, "What's the shooting about?"

Jim walked toward them, more angry now than scared. He was thinking of Ann Dunn who would get everything his father had owned if he died before the year was up. Well, tonight was as good as any for her to make her fortune. Anyone could have fired those shots. The chances were Monte Smith had told everybody in town that Jim Dunn had got off the train.

"I was getting my welcome home," Jim said as he came into the light, "but not the kind of welcome I cotton to."

42

"Jim Dunn," Royal said as if completely surprised.

The rest backed away, Monte Smith among them. Only fat Rafferty stepped up and held out his hand. "Sure glad to see you, Jim. Now who the hell would want to plug you the first night you're in town?"

Jim shook his head, looking past Rafferty at Royal, a small, colorless man who had lived in fear of Sherm Dunn. Jim, still looking at Royal, said, "I'd like to know, Raff. I sure would."

Royal said, "Hank Watrous will be along. He'll look into it."

"Come in," Rafferty said. "I'll set 'em up. You oughtta have a better welcome than you just had."

Rafferty lumbered through the bat wings, Jim following, the others stringing along behind. Jim set his valise down, took off his hat and ran a finger through the bullet hole in the crown. "It was that close," he said. Without warning, he wheeled toward Monte Smith, grabbed him by the front of his dirty shirt and shook him. "Who'd you tell I got off the train?"

Smith yelped and tried to break free. His shirt ripped as he backtracked toward the door, leaving Jim standing by the bar with both hands clutching fragments of Smith's shirt. "Nobody, Jim. So help me." He kept on backing up, stumbled as he reached the step-down to the walk and sprawled on his back. He got up, cursing, and limped away into the darkness.

43

The rest left, all but Royal and Rafferty who set out a bottle of Old Crow and three glasses. Rafferty poured the drinks and placed the bottle on the bar. "Been a long time since I had a drink," he said. "This is a special occasion."

Uncertainly Royal reached for his, muttered, "Here's mud in your eye," and they drank together.

Jim said, "You got a busted window."

"I ain't worried about that. I'm just glad you didn't get hit," Royal replied.

To Jim's ears the storeman's tone carried no sincerity. They waited, the silence uneasy, and presently Hank Watrous came in, sleepy and tired and cranky. He looked at Jim distastefully and licked dry lips. "So you're back in town. I guess you had to let off a little steam."

Again anger crowded Jim. He didn't know Watrous well and he had no idea how he happened to be wearing the sheriff's star, but at the moment he could not think of anyone who would be more useless as a law man. "They sure scraped the bottom of the barrel when they gave you the star, Hank. Better start earning your pay."

Watrous' old-young face turned red. "You're damned right I'll earn it. Give me your gun. I'll throw you into the jug to cool off till morning. Even if your name is Dunn, you ain't . . . ."

"Come and get my gun if you want it," Jim said.

"Hold on, Hank," Rafferty broke in. "You're going off half-cocked like always. Someone tried to kill Jim while he was walking along the street. Tell him about it, Jim."

"No use," Jim said. "He hasn't got sense enough to understand it if I talked a week."

"Cut it out, both of you," Rafferty said testily. "How about it, Hank? You going to start looking?"

"Where?" Watrous asked. "Whoever did it wouldn't leave no calling card."

"I've heard about a gent named Colter who might have reason for wanting me out of the way," Jim said.

"He's one man I know didn't do it," Watrous said. "I was talking to him when I heard the shots." He scratched his nose, an idea apparently breaking through his tired brain. "Now that I think about it, me and Colter was talking about Frank Castleman. He's had it in for Dunn here ever since that poker game and everybody knows it."

"Not Frank," Royal said hotly. "He's the best worker I ever had in the store. He . . ."

Royal stopped, embarrassed, and reached for the bottle. Jim said softly, "Remember something, maybe, Bill?"

Royal was silent. Rafferty said, "Sure, Hank, we've all heard Frank talk, but we figured it was just talk. Maybe you better see if you can find him, though. Won't hurt."

Watrous, glum-faced, walked out. Royal took his drink, said, "See you tomorrow, Jim," and left the saloon.

Rafferty pushed the bottle at Jim. "Have another one."

Jim shook his head. "One's the limit for me."

Rafferty scratched his third chin back. "Well now, you take the pledge?"

"No, I just got smart. I haven't had more'n one drink in a day since I left here."

Rafferty nodded approvingly. "Maybe you'll amount to something, Jim. When you left here, I didn't figger you would."

"There's something I'd like to know," Jim said. "I get the idea Watrous would just as soon I'd have got plugged. The rest of 'em too."

Rafferty carefully set the bottle of Old Crow back on the shelf and walking to the end of the bar, lifted the cover of the cigar case and helped himself. He came back, chewing on the cigar. He said, "Kind of hard to tell you, Jim, but things ain't like they were when you left. Sherm, well, he changed. Seemed like he got greedy. Anyhow, the bank started putting the screws on some of the little fry. Several farmers like Watrous lost their places. More of 'em would have if Sherm hadn't cashed in."

Rafferty hunched his fat shoulders, a forefinger making circles on the bar. "Folks will think of Sherm the way he was just before he died, and they'll forget a hell of a lot of generous things he done when he was younger." He looked up. "Another thing, Jim. They'll remember you as an

46

ornery hellion no matter what you are now or what you're gonna be. You won't have it easy, Jim."

Jim rolled a smoke and lighted it. Both were silent, Rafferty watching Jim uncertainly, and Jim thinking about what Rafferty had said. He had never considered his father greedy. It all went back to the woman Sherm Dunn had married. It must, and yet Jim couldn't quite make things jibe. His father had spent a large part of his life making his name mean something, then he got old and fell in love with a young woman and he completely changed. No, it didn't jibe, and yet who could say what a man over sixty might do to make a young, attractive woman love him?

"What's Dad's wife like, Raff?" Jim asked. "The widow, I mean."

Rafferty had been chewing on a cold cigar, now he made a show of digging a match out of his vest pocket and lighting it. Finally he said, "I ain't the man to ask, Jim. All I can say is that I see her drive into town with Maggie O'Boyle, or sometimes with Bud Colter. She shops in the Mercantile or the jewelry store, has dinner in the hotel, and goes back to the Box D, lonesome as hell or I miss my guess."

"What about the women in town? Does she have any friends?"

"No, she don't." Rafferty took the cigar out of his mouth and studied it. "There's a lot of gossip

47

which is natural, Sherm fetching in a purty thing like he done. You know, Jim, I'm glad I'm a bachelor. Women who are supposed to be good women can be mighty damned mean, and they have been to Miz Dunn."

Watrous came in, his steps dragging. "I didn't figure it was Frank. He was in bed which is where I oughtta be, and he was mighty put out 'cause I woked him up. Said he had to get up early in the morning to unload some freight for Bill Royal."

"You look at his Winchester?" Jim asked.

"Sure. Hadn't been fired. Hanging right by the door like it always is."

That didn't prove anything to Jim. Castleman could own two rifles, but Jim knew he would only irritate Watrous if he raised the point. The sheriff was walking toward the bat wings, plainly done with the whole business.

"Hold on," Jim called. Watrous turned, putting a hand on the bar to steady himself. "Monte Smith saw me get off the train and he lit out like a dog with a can on his tail. You go find out who he told I got off the train."

Watrous screwed up his face as if he were so tired that it took a moment for Jim's words to unravel and make sense. He said, "Monte'll be around tomorrow. I've got to get home. Got a sick baby."

He went out and this time Jim let him go. He said, "You elected yourself quite a sheriff. I

48

suppose he's doubling as town marshal, too."

"Sure," Rafferty said. "Cairo can't afford a full salary. You know how your dad was 'bout taxes. Judge Riddle and Doc Finley ain't no better."

Jim picked up his valise. "Thanks for the drink, Raff."

Rafferty said, "Watch yourself when you get out to the Box D. Don't make no mistakes just because Bud Colter is a purty boy."

"I'll watch it," Jim said, and went out.

"Jim."

It was Ginny, waiting on the walk for him. He went to her, putting down his valise and taking her hands. He asked, "What have I come back to, Ginny?"

"I tried to tell you," she said, "but you wouldn't listen. I heard the shots. Were they fired at you?"

"I guess so, but they were wild," he said as if it didn't matter. He looked at her in the thin light and he thought how much he loved her and what he had to do before he could have her. He said softly, "Don't worry about me. I'll be all right. Just wait for six months. I love you, but I've got to go ahead. Can you understand?"

"Of course," she said, "but I'm afraid for you. Most of all I'm afraid of that woman."

She kissed him, and turning, walked away into the darkness. He picked up his valise and went on to the hotel. Tomorrow he would see Ann Dunn.

CHAPTER V

Bud Colter reached the foot of the mesa hill south of town before it occurred to him that Monte Smith was, or might be, dangerous. Colter wasn't whistling now. The more he thought about Smith, the less he felt like whistling. He reined up, turning it over in his mind. As far as he personally was concerned, he had the best alibi a man could have, but that wasn't the whole point.

The trouble was it would be hard to convict Castleman of murder in a Cairo court. On the other hand, Colter had no illusions about one thing. People would wonder about Sherm Dunn's death, they would wonder more about Jim's, and when Colter married Ann . . . ! Why, the whole damned country would buzz.

Everyone knew there were men among the Box D crew who would do anything he told them, including murder. Monte Smith would be the first to tell he had brought word to Colter that Jim Dunn was in town, and that would point the minds of suspicious men like Judge Riddle in a direction Colter wouldn't like.

For a long moment he sat in his saddle, caught in a trap of indecision. He had no qualms about committing another murder. The question was one of picking the best odds. Monte Smith would talk. That much was certain. But would his talking incriminate Colter? Then he thought of Ann, how much she valued security and respectability, and he made his choice. Smith's testimony might mean nothing, but it was better not to take any chances.

As he turned his horse back to town, he admitted to himself, and it hurt his pride to do it, that Ann Dunn was fashioning his thoughts. He had always been able to get what he wanted from women. There was no reason for Ann to be any different, but she was. When this was all wound up, with Ann in possession of every nickel old Sherm had, she might say to hell with Bud Colter.

He swore. He'd break her damned pretty neck if she took that attitude. He'd put her where she was. But this was poor thinking and he found no comfort in it. The truth was he would kill a man because he saw a slim chance that man might turn Ann against him by bringing him under suspicion in the eyes of the community.

By keeping to alleys and back streets, Colter reached the one-room shack in the east end of town where Smith lived, feeling reasonably sure he had not been seen. He wouldn't be recognized anyhow, as dark as it was. He dismounted, and leaving the horse behind the shack, walked around it and shoved the door open. He said, "Monte." There was no answer. He pulled his gun and drew it quickly across the dirty blankets. No one was there.

Colter walked around the bunk and stood with his back against the wall, facing the door. Smith would probably hang around Rafferty's saloon as long as he could, or at least as long as he had any hope of sponging a drink off someone. But Rafferty closed at midnight and Smith would surely come home then.

So Colter waited, the minutes dragging out. He strangled an impulse to look at his watch. He'd have to light a match, and he didn't want to risk warning Smith. Then, it might have been ten minutes, or twenty, Colter had no way of telling, he heard Smith's scuffing gait as the man came along the road. He reached the door, muttering something, and struck a match.

Colter fired twice. After the hammering sounds of the shots had died, doubly loud here in the confines of the small room, Colter heard a long, drawn-out gurgling sound, then there was silence. Crossing to the doorway, he found Smith lying with his feet inside the cabin, his head out, stone dead.

Quickly Colter stepped over the body, ran around the shack, and mounting, rode away. He laughed silently, wondering what Watrous would say when someone woke him out of the stupor of sleep and reported another shooting.

Colter crossed Ruby Mesa and took the looping

road down into Ouray Valley, letting his horse have his head, for it was black dark, and Colter, if he had been afoot, would probably have fallen off the edge of the cliff. He tried to get his thoughts back to Ann and the way it would be after they were married. He'd be the big man he had always dreamed of being. No more penny ante stuff. No more bank robbing and running and hiding and wondering if he'd run into a posse just around the next bend. But somehow he couldn't make it work. Smith's killing had been an unpleasant interlude that had destroyed the highly satisfactory mood he'd been in when he'd left Hank Watrous.

Colter had intended to wake Ann when he reached the Box D and tell her Jim Dunn was in town, but that she didn't have to worry. He looked at his watch after he unsaddled and let his horse into the corral. It was after two. He'd better wait until morning.

After he was stretched out in his bunk, he found that he could not sleep. One thing after another ran through his mind until he finally remembered how he had stood at the bar when Smith walked in and had come directly at him and a moment later he had asked Rafferty to pour a drink for his friend Monte Smith.

Rafferty would remember he'd talked to Smith and Rafferty would tell Watrous. He should have killed Rafferty, too, before he'd left town. And Watrous. Why, he'd sat right there in the sheriff's front room and told him Dunn was back. After a while Watrous would think of it and wonder how he'd known about Dunn being on the train.

That was the trouble with murder. One led to another and sooner or later you made a mistake. He should have stopped with old Sherm Dunn. Well, it didn't make much difference one way or the other about Monte Smith. But he'd been jumpy or he wouldn't have gone back and beefed Smith. That was bad. He'd seen it happen plenty of times, men who had reached out and put the rope around their necks by getting too anxious.

He lay on his back listening to Alec Torrin's snoring. Stubborn old fool, Alec was. Colter had got rid of the rest of them, all except the cook who didn't cut any ice and Lennie Nolan who was in the line cabin on the divide. He'd have fired all of them if Ann had let him. Well, they'd go as soon as they heard about Jim Dunn.

Presently it was daylight and Colter had not slept at all. He got up with the crew, dressed, and washed outside, the dawn October air very crisp and bringing with it a harsh promise of winter. He was glad roundup was over. You never knew about weather in this country. Better be early than wearing your horse out in snow up to his belly.

He ate with the others, studying them covertly. Toy Severe was small for ranch work, but he was willing enough and he was hell on wheels with the Peacemaker he carried wherever he went. The

Mason boys? Well, not very smart, but loyal as long as they smelled a few dollars coming their way. Crip Lannigen? He wasn't very smart, either, not like Severe, but he was a good fighting man.

This was probably the longest spell of honest work they had done in their lives, Colter told himself. When he took over here, he'd thought he would need them, but he hadn't, and now he wished he was rid of them. He'd made big promises, too big, and he was going to have to find a way to deliver before long.

He gave the orders for the day. The Mason boys to keep on working with the rough string. Lannigen to take salt up to the Rabbit Creek range. Torrin to clean out the first corral. "What the hell you been doing lately, Alec?" he demanded. He liked to rawhide Torrin because the old cowhand kept saying things would be different when Jim Dunn got back. He went on, "You been sitting on that wheelbarrow behind the barn, ain't you? Well, today you'd better push it." He grinned as he saw the familiar, tight-lipped expression come into Torrin's face. The old boy would spool his cotton and be on his way before sundown.

Colter nodded at Toy Severe. "Saddle up for me. We're taking a look at the Monument Rock range. We may have to start bringing that she stuff down in a few days."

He wheeled and strode into the house. Ann would still be asleep, but he'd get her up. If she was going to be a ranch woman, it was time she was learning to get up in the morning. Sherm had sure spoiled her. He thought about the old days when she'd sung for a living in saloons from Texas to California, showing off her legs and giving the boys a promise she had no intention of fulfilling. He'd never dreamed he'd see her settled down on a spread like the Box D with a bank thrown into the deal to boot. He grinned. Neither had she.

When he went in through the front door, he heard Maggie O'Boyle banging around in the kitchen. He called, "Ann up yet?"

Maggie lumbered into the front room, scowling. She was a large woman with arms bigger than an average man's thighs, wide hips and ample breasts that had become tired with the years and now sagged despondently. Her hair that had once been fiery red was quite gray. She was a hard worker, she had the devil's own temper when it was aroused, and she despised Bud Colter.

"Mrs. Dunn to you, you spalpeen," she said. "No, she ain't up. No reason why she should be."

"I'll get her up," Colter said. "I want to see her before I ride out."

"You will do no such thing, Bud Colter." Seeing that he had started up the stairs, she stomped across the room, her big hands swinging at her sides. "I'm warning you, Bud. You so much as put a knuckle to the door of Mrs. Dunn's room and I'll take that purty mustache of yours and twist it around your throat and choke you to death, so help me."

Colter was within one step of the top of the stairs. He stopped, a hand on the oak banister, and looked down at her. She stood at the foot, glaring up at him, her big face red with anger, her whiskery upper lip trembling. Colter swung around and came down.

"Maggie, I believe you'd do it," he said.

"You know I would," she said. "Some men never learn their places, so women like me have to teach 'em."

He chucked her under the chin. "One of these days I'm going to marry you, Maggie," he said, and walked out.

"The day they dance on my coffin," she flung after him.

He didn't look back. He walked to the corral, mounted the sorrel Severe had saddled for him, and started south, saying nothing to the little gunman who fell in behind him. There was something about this situation that worried him, something he couldn't quite put his fingers on. At times he wondered if old Sherm Dunn's ghost still lingered around the Box D. Maggie O'Boyle certainly had his spirit. So did Alec Torrin and Lennie Nolan and Sugar Sanders.

Well, he could stand it until they heard about Jim Dunn. They were all waiting for him to come back, waiting to see what kind of man he'd turned out to be. All of them were sure that in time he would come back.

There was a loyalty here he couldn't understand, a loyalty that did not depend upon high wages or the promise of a reward to come. It was something rare, and good. Bud Colter, who had no understanding of goodness, sensed that.

When they topped the south rim, Severe rode up beside Colter. He said, "Bud, the boys are getting restless. What are your plans?"

Colter glared at the fox-faced little man. His lack of sleep and his failure to see Ann this morning caught up with him and turned him irritable. He said crossly, "No plans, damn it. We've got six more months to wait. This is a good enough place to winter, ain't it?"

"No," Severe said. "Your promises are like the hole in a doughnut, Bud. Is there anything around the hole?"

He didn't need Severe or any of them now, he told himself. When you were the husband of the owner of the Box D, you didn't keep a tough crew like this. But he didn't tell Severe that. The little man had a touchy pride. This needed time and thought, so he said mildly, "I'll see what I can do, Toy."

Chapter VI

Jim woke at sunup long before the town stirred. He lay on his back as the sun destroyed the last of the night shadows that lingered in the corners of the room, a room that was little different from any of a dozen rooms in a dozen towns he had seen in the last three years. Torn wallpaper, dirty windows, the rickety pine bureau, the paint-peeled bedstead, the single rawhide bottom chair, and the drawings and scrawled verses on the wall, some pornographic and some simply insipid. He wondered how many men had slept in this room, drifters with no roots whatever to hold them, men who would work a few days here and a few there, ride the grub line from one ranch to another, and finally die and be buried in unmarked graves.

He got up and dressed. He had been reviewing his own life, he thought, the life he would have lived if Judge Riddle hadn't sent for him. For all of his good intentions, he would never have come back. But now there would be no more drifting for Jim Dunn. The Box D belonged to him. To get it, all he had to do was to live out there for six months in the same house with a woman he would hate.

The first thing he'd do would be to get rid of Bud Colter and the tough hands who made up his crew. He didn't care what Ann Dunn thought of it. He'd send her packing, too, as soon as he could. The chances were he'd never get any evidence proving that Colter had murdered Sherman Dunn. It wouldn't do any good if he could, with a poor stick like Hank Watrous packing the star, but at least he'd get them out of the way.

He went down stairs and had to wait in the lobby until the dining room was open. When he finished breakfast, he stepped into the street. For a time he stood in front of the hotel, soaking in the early morning sunshine.

Now that it was daylight, he could see little difference in Main Street from the time he had left the country. Dust hock deep on a horse, the rickety boardwalks that dated back to the time Sherm Dunn and Judge Riddle had founded the town, the false fronts claiming pretentiousness for Cairo that was sheer mockery.

Across from the hotel was a brick building, the only one in town. Above the door and windows was a large sign with the words, CAIRO STATE BANK, and below it in smaller letters, Sherman Dunn, Pres. He was dead but he was still here in many ways, Jim thought, and he would be for years to come.

Some men died and were buried and the next day were forgotten. But not Sherman Dunn. Every living person had a little different picture of him. Jim pondered that thought, wondering if his memory of his father was distorted by his youth and therefore was wrong. Would it have been different if he could have seen his father again, bringing to that meeting the maturity of three years of independent living? He didn't know.

He turned toward the livery stable. He had no reason to remain in town. He was putting off seeing Ann Dunn just as a man would put off going to a doctor or a dentist because he knew the visit would be painful. You could kill a man, but what could you do with a woman you wanted to kill?

Shep Hofferd, the liveryman, knew him at once, but he made no effort to shake hands. He said, "Howdy, Jim," as if Jim had not been gone at all. No cordiality. No hostility, either.

"I want a horse, Shep," Jim said, "and a saddle that's not completely shot."

Hofferd had heard he was back, Jim thought. There had been a day when Hofferd would have shaken hands with him just as Rafferty had last night, but this wasn't the day. Hofferd simply turned and walked down the runway.

A few minutes later the stableman returned with a brown gelding. He said, "Monte Smith was shot and killed last night. You heard?"

"No."

Fear clawed up through Jim as he realized he had no alibi if he was accused. He had gone to the hotel and taken a room when he had left Rafferty, but there was a back stairs to the hotel. It would have been easy enough to go down to the alley and come back after he had killed Smith. He had no motive, but there were some who might think he had, Royal and Rafferty and the rest of them who had seen him tear Smith's shirt the night before in the saloon.

Hofferd was watching him closely. Now he said, "There's talk you might have done it. Don't seem to me you had much reason, but nobody else did, neither. Old Monte wasn't no good and he wasn't bad."

Without a word Jim mounted and rode out of the barn, making no denial to Hofferd. Why should he? Then, reaching the corner of the block, he decided he wasn't ready to leave town. The man who had shot at him must have been the one who had killed Smith. There could be only one reason for killing a man like Smith: he knew something the murderer was afraid he'd tell. That something could have been the fatal knowledge of the identity of the man Smith had gone to with the information Jim Dunn was in town. So, following that line of reasoning, Jim arrived at Frank Castleman.

He turned up the alley until he reached the rear of Bill Royal's Mercantile. Leaving the gelding ground hitched, he walked up the ramp to the loading platform and went into the big back room that served as a warehouse for Royal. Frank Castleman was piling sacks of flour against the wall.

Jim said, "Howdy, Frank."

Castleman jumped and wheeled to face Jim, then began backing away. Jim followed slowly, his eyes on Castleman's face. He looked guilty, Jim thought, but knew it might be his imagination. They moved that way, Castleman retreating, Jim advancing, until Castleman bumped into the wall between the store and the back room.

Castleman said, his voice trembling, "If you're going to kill me, get it over with."

"Got a gun?"

"No."

"Then get one."

"No." Castleman stood with his back against the wall, breathing hard. "We've heard about you. Killed a couple of men since you left. A hardcase, now ain't you, Dunn? Well, I'll give you no excuse to plug me. If you shoot an unarmed man in this town, they'll hang you in spite of God and Judge Riddle."

"You shot Monte Smith last night, didn't you?" Jim asked. "Shot him to keep him from telling that you were the one he went to after he saw me get off the train."

"Not me." Then, apparently sure that Jim wasn't going to shoot him, Castleman took a step forward. "I've got something to say to you, mister.

63

You made a mistake coming back. Your old man and Judge Riddle have run this town long enough. Somebody got rid of Sherm and somebody will do the same to Riddle." He tapped his chest. "And I'll get rid of you."

Jim could not make out Castleman's face clearly here in the gloom of the storeroom, but he sensed the feral hatred that was in the man, the brooding and bitterness that had burned out what had been decent in Frank Castleman. He had known before he'd left that Castleman hated him, but not like this, so warped and twisted he was not the Frank Castleman Jim had known.

"Why, Frank?" Jim asked gently. "You think I crooked you in that poker game we played four years ago?"

"No, you didn't crook me," Castleman said, "but everything was too damned pat. You and Sherm and the Judge and the bank." He took another step toward Jim. "High and mighty, Sherm and the Judge. They just talked to God and once in awhile to Doc Finley. The rest of us, me'n Hank Watrous and everybody else, we wasn't even fit to own our places. Sherm, he used the bank to steal our land. Then he marries that damned floozy and tries to shove her down the throat of every decent woman in the county, and when he couldn't do it, he got worse."

Castleman stopped his tirade because he was out of breath. His hatred was like a terrible stench in the air. Jim said, "It was Dad you should have gone after, not me."

"Your name's Dunn, ain't it?" Castleman took another step, until he was within ten feet of Jim. "You got my ranch in the poker game. That's enough to kill you for." He swallowed. "I had a ranch. I never bothered anybody. I worked hard and I'd have made a go of it if I'd had a chance. But I didn't. In this town you get more if you've got a lot. If you don't have much, you get less. I should have killed you when you were here, but I didn't have the guts then. So I've been waiting, working my head off for Bill Royal. I don't have no fun. I just eat and sleep and work, and all the time I've been waiting for you to come back."

"So you tried last night," Jim said.

Castleman glanced behind him to see if anyone had come in from the store. Then he said in a low tone, "That's right, only don't bother to tell Watrous because I'll deny it. It was too damned dark to shoot straight. I should have waited till you got in front of the saloon, but all of a sudden it seemed like I'd been waiting too long and I couldn't wait no longer, so I let go, then I got scared soon as you shot 'cause I knew I'd missed."

"Go get a gun and we'll try it again," Jim said.

"I told you no," Castleman whispered. "I'll get you when you ain't expecting it. From some rim, maybe, when you're riding down into a canyon.

Or walking along Main Street after dark like you was last night. You won't know when to expect it or how it'll come, and all the time you'll be eating your guts out wondering when and how."

He grabbed an ax that had been leaning against the wall and jumped at Jim, swinging the ax at Jim's head. He had been talking to gain this opportunity, and in the thin light of the storeroom, Jim had not even seen the ax. He dropped to his knees as the sharp edge swept over his head.

Close, as close as Castleman's bullet had come last night. He came up off his knees, lunging straight at Castleman who was pulled off balance when the ax missed. Jim hit him on the side of the head, swiveling it half around on the muscular neck, then he brought his left through to Castleman's belly, doubling him over in agony.

Jim twisted the ax out of his hands and threw it across the storeroom. He heard it hit a pile of pots and pans, banging and clattering as it slid to the floor. Royal came running in from the store yelling, "What's going on? What's going on?"

Jim had no time to discuss his current project. He hit Castleman in the face again and knocked him flat on his back. He jumped onto him, and grabbing him by the hair, banged his head against the floor. Castleman, only half conscious, rammed a hand against Jim's face and pushed. He threshed from one side to the other, tried to bring his knees up against Jim's back, but there was no real power in his blows. He jammed his other hand up, his thumb extended, trying to catch Jim's right eye but missed by an inch, his thumb striking the cheekbone.

Royal had Jim by the shoulder and was shaking him, screaming, "Stop it, Dunn, stop it. You trying to kill another man?"

Jim might have killed him. He was never really sure, for he was half out of his head with rage. He had his hands on the man who had tried to kill him last night and had tried again just now with an ax, a man who would keep on trying until he succeeded or was killed.

Slowly Royal's words penetrated his brain and he realized this was not the time, that it would be murder in the eyes of the people of Cairo. He was holding Castleman's head off the floor. He let go and got up, hearing the man's head hit the boards with a sharp rap.

"He admitted he tried to shoot me last night," Jim said. "He came at me just now with an ax. What do you want me to do, let him keep it up till he does the job?"

Castleman tried to sit up and fell back. He muttered, "He's lying, Bill. Lying like a dog."

"That's what I figured," Royal said, "coming in the back like he done."

"Any crime in that?" Jim demanded. "I wanted to talk to Castleman and I thought he'd be back here."

"You mean you wanted to kill him," Royal said
hotly. "You were a bad one before, Jim, drinking
and brawling around like a wild man, but you
weren't a mad dog killer. Now looks to me like
you are."

No good, Jim thought as he looked at the little
storekeeper, no good at all. He hadn't come in
here for this. He looked down at Castleman's
bruised and bloody face, then at Royal's that was
the picture of indignation, and now, calmed a
little, he remembered all that Castleman had said
about his father.

"This town looks the same as when I left," Jim
said, "but it's not the same at all. Frank was giving
Dad hell. He's got no reason . . ."

"He had plenty of reason," Royal said. "Maybe
most of us don't go around talking like Frank
done, but we feel the same way."

"Why?" Jim demanded.

"Because a bank should be a servant of the
people and he used it for a club to steal their land."
Royal swallowed, fury building in him, and then,
with a little man's spitefulness, he added, "And all
of us had to bow and scrape in front of him. Now
you're back and I suppose you figure you'll pick
up . . ."

Jim whirled and walked out. There was no use
to listen to that. He mounted and rode out of
town, crossing the bridge that spanned the
Uncompahgre and heading south through tall

walls of chico brush that crowded the road. Then the last of the houses were behind him and he looked up at the sky that was totally blue, and he thought what a little, spiteful, tawdry town Cairo was, turning against Sherman Dunn now that he was dead. If felt good just to be out of it.

CHAPTER VII

When Jim reached Ruby Mesa he had, for the first time, a feeling he had come home. Here was the land laid out for him to see. He reined up in the middle of the road and smoked a cigarette, and it occurred to him that in all the years he had lived here as a boy, he had never really seen this country, at least not with the eyes that he saw it with now.

Grand Mesa lay to the north, a great, flat-topped mountain with its myriad of lakes and streams, the crest of it a level line running on and on for miles until it broke off sharply to his left. The Uncompahgre Plateau was on the west, the divide as it was commonly called, its gently lifting slope covered by quaking asps and spruce, Box D's summer range.

To the south were the San Juans, their granite saw teeth scraping the sky. An early snow had already frosted the tips of the great peaks. Behind him were the 'dobe hills, the lower slopes almost without vegetation. They lay gray and forbidding under the sharp October sun, their countless ridges and gullies the result of centuries of erosion. Now they looked like a giant washboard turned over on its side.

He rode on, his shortening shadow keeping pace with him, a little sick now as he thought how different this was going to be from what he had mentally pictured so many times. He was the prodigal son, and his father, in spite of the fury that had ruled him when Jim had left, would have welcomed him back just as the prodigal's father had once welcomed him.

But now there was no father. Only the widow who may have been the cause of her husband's death and had very likely been responsible for the shooting last night. Perhaps she was paying Frank Castleman to continue his insane efforts to exact vengeance for a fancied wrong. This was a new and startling thought, and yet it made sense out of an attempted murder that up to now had made very little sense.

Judge Riddle had said the woman would get a cash settlement if Jim made a success out of the ranch. He hadn't said how much, but big or little, she would certainly want more if she could get it. There were two things she could do: see that Jim Dunn died before the six months was up, or make it impossible for him to succeed with the ranch.

She couldn't manage the latter if he got rid of Colter and his hardcase crew; the former she could do by using Frank Castleman or anyone else who would shoot straight for a price.

So he reached the south edge of Ruby Mesa and rode down the narrow switchbacks to the valley, prepared to hate Ann Dunn and deal with her as harshly as he could. Then, looking ahead at the buildings that had been his boyhood home, he momentarily forgot the woman. He fully expected to find the Box D in the worst, run-down condition he had ever seen it, for Bud Colter would certainly not be the foreman Luke Dilly had been.

He had been completely mistaken. The house was shiny with new white paint. The corrals were in good shape. Usually a great deal of junk littered the yard: wire, lumber, wagons, machinery, and the various odds and ends that gather around a working ranch. Now the place looked clean and neat. A new shed south of the house had apparently been built to protect the ranch equipment from the weather.

He rode slowly across the valley to the buildings, the haystacks scattered along the creek indicating that the hay crop had been a good one. Two men were working with a horse in one of the far corrals. Another man was cleaning out the corral next to the barn, and when Jim rode into the yard, he saw it was Alec Torrin.

The first thing he'd do would be to fire Bud

Colter. That would not be easy if Colter was half the man everyone in town seemed to think he was. Perhaps it would be better to see Ann Dunn first, then he decided against it. He'd start with Alec. There was a good chance Colter wasn't even around the place at this time of day.

If Jim was seen riding in, there was no indication of it. All three men went right on with what they were doing. Jim dismounted, leaving his reins hanging, and walked toward Torrin who had just finished loading the wheelbarrow and was starting toward the gate with it.

Jim called, "How are you, Alec?"

Torrin set the wheelbarrow down and straightened, wiping a sleeve across his sweaty forehead. For a moment he stared at Jim, then he let out a whoop. "Jim! Damned if it ain't." He ran toward Jim in his floundering, bowlegged way, his hand extended. "Boy, I ain't seen nothing in all my life as purty as your ugly face."

He pumped Jim's hand and slapped him on the back, and tears began running down his seamed, leathery cheeks. He looked away, shamefaced, muttering, "Sure been sweating today," and wiped his sleeve across his face again.

Jim didn't feel like talking, either. He stood there, staring at Alec Torrin, not old by most standards but old as cowhands went, reduced to chore boy on the ranch he had helped Sherman Dunn and Luke Dilly and the rest of them build. He knew all there was to know, or so it had seemed to Jim when he'd been a boy, but whether that was true or not, he was sure of one thing. He owed more to old Alec than any other living man.

"Let's get around into the shade," Jim said. "I've got some questions to ask."

"Sure, son." Alec blew his nose on his red bandanna and moved around to the shady side of the barn. "When did you get in?"

"Last night on the ten o'clock." They squatted in the shade, Jim rolling a cigarette, and when he glanced up at Alec, he was shocked by two things. Alec had aged ten years in these three, and he was looking at Jim as if he were God and now all things could be done.

"You look good, boy," Alec said. "You're bigger'n when you left, and you look tough enough to handle this outfit." He licked his lips and swallowed. "You're going to, ain't you?"

"If I live," Jim said. "What kind of a huckleberry is this Colter I've been hearing about?"

"Tough and mean." Alec's face turned bitter as the memories of a thousand indignities rushed into his mind. "I've stayed on 'cause I knowed you'd come back, but I was about to give up. Colter piles it onto me. When Lennie comes down off the divide, he'll get the same, but Maggie, she don't see much of him. She's got him buffaloed anyhow, looks like. Far as Sugar goes, Colter can't bother him much as long as he puts out the grub. That's

73

what we've all stayed for, Jim, just hopin' you'd come back."

Jim stared at the two-story ranch house with the row of cottonwoods in front of it, the leaves turning in the wind that breathed up the valley, some of them yellow, and he could not remember when he had felt like crying the way he did now, just putting his head down and bawling.

He had always liked Alec, but looking back, he realized it had been in a half-hearted way, not what Alec had deserved. And Maggie. Lennie. Old Sugar, too. Sugar who used to slip him a whole pie to eat when no one was around. But this business of hanging on to help hold the ranch until he came back was something that was hard to understand. He would have dismissed it lightly when he'd left, but now it meant a great deal to him.

"Thanks, Alec," he said finally. "I can't tell you how I feel about that. But I'm not the same Jim Dunn who went away. I want you to know that."

"I can see it," Alec said. "And I want you to know something. We'll help you all we can." He got a short-stemmed briar pipe out of his pocket and filled it. "But there's five of 'em, and they're a bad bunch. A good crew as you can see by looking around. Plenty of hay. Cattle in good shape. Never knew things to be better, but that ain't the point."

Jim nodded. "What about the widow?"

Alec sighed. "Talk to Maggie, Jim. All I can say

is that Miz Dunn is a fine woman. Except when he'd get to thinking about you, Sherm was never happier in his life than after he got married."

"What's between her and Colter?"

"Nothing, except that she asked Sherm to hire the bastard. She knew what she was doing, too. I hate to say it, but he's a better cowman than Luke Dilly ever was."

Jim was irritated to hear anything good about Ann Dunn, and yet he should have expected it. A woman who could get around his father could do as much with Alec Torrin.

"Did Colter murder Dad?" Jim asked.

Alec stared at his pipe. "That I dunno."

"But you think so, don't you?"

"I just dunno."

Jim flipped his cigarette stub into the dust of the yard. Of course Alec didn't know. If he did, he would have gone to Watrous. He was not one to accuse a man of murder unless he knew, even a man he hated as much as he hated Bud Colter.

"Where are his crew and what are they doing?" Jim asked.

"The Mason boys are in the back corral." Alec jerked a thumb over his shoulder. "Crip Lannigen took some salt up to Rabbit Creek. Colter and Toy Severe rode out together. Dunno where."

"Toy Severe? The gun fighter?"

"That's him. Weasel mean, he is. I dunno why he's here. He could get twice as much money for his gun than Box D pays him."

Jim nodded. He had never seen the man, but he had crossed his path several times in New Mexico and Texas, and not once had he heard a good word about him. Severe had killed four men in a range war in southern Texas and barely got out with his life. Box D was comparatively isolated here on Colorado's western slope. It was possible Toy Severe was using it for a hideout until the Texas trouble cooled off.

"I'm going to fire the bunch," Jim said as he rose, "and I'm going to do it today."

Alec got up. "What do you figure to use for a crew this winter?"

"Won't need much of a crew."

"You'll need more crew'n you think," Alec said. "And there's one thing you don't know. You'll have a hell of a time getting a crew around here."

"I'll put you and Maggie and Sugar in the saddle if I have to," Jim glanced at the sun. "Dinner time. The Mason boys ought to be coming in about now, hadn't they?"

"I reckon." Alec stepped to the corner of the barn. "They've started."

"We'll begin with them," Jim said.

Alec scratched his chin and nodded. Jim sensed his doubts. The Jim Dunn Alec had known three years ago could not have handled two men tough enough to work for Bud Colter, let alone Colter himself and a gunman like Toy Severe. This, Jim knew, was the test. He'd send the Masons packing, or he was whipped before he started.

Jim drew his gun and stepped back into the stable. He said, "Talk to 'em a minute. I don't want to kill 'em if I can help it."

The doubts plainly lingered in Alec's mind, but he made no objections. He remained in the shade of the barn, lighting his pipe as the Masons rounded the corner of the barn. They were in their late twenties, big, swarthy men who would have weighed in close to two hundred pounds.

The older one, Ash, said, "Quit a mite early, didn't you, Torrin?"

The other, Del, younger by two years and follower of his brother, said, "Bud'll work you over, Torrin. Remember what he said when he left this morning."

They were facing Alec, both reaching for tobacco and paper and grinning like two oversized tomcats, when Jim stepped out of the stable. "You're fired and you're sloping out of here pronto," he said. "If there's anything in the bunkhouse you want, get it and drift."

Their hands dropped to their sides as their mouths sagged open, but they didn't touch gun butts. They glanced at the brown gelding, they looked at Alec and then at Jim, and for a moment they seemed absolutely at a loss as to what to do or say.

Alec let the silence ribbon out, then he said,

77

"This is Jim Dunn. He's taking the Box D over and he's starting today."

Ash Mason began to swear and stopped when Jim said, "Hit the dirt."

"What do you think will happen when Bud gets in?" Ash demanded. "He won't stand for getting fired. And what about Miz Dunn? She's got something to say . . ."

"Friend," Jim said, "I'll give you five seconds and then I'll start shooting."

They looked at his lean face, then at the gun held as steady as death in his right hand, and without another word turned back to the corral. They roped and saddled their horses, Jim and Alec watching in silence, and after they mounted, Ash said, "Your hand today, Dunn. There's always another deal."

Jim slipped his gun into the holster. If they wanted to make a fight out of it, they could, but they were in the saddle now, and even with the odds favoring them, they wanted none of it. Jim said, "When there's another deal, I'll get a new hand, too."

"We'll be in Cairo," Ash said. "Tell Bud if he comes to town . . ." A quick grin touched his lips. "Only I figure it'll be you who shows up in town, not Bud."

"And you'd better be packing that iron," Del said.

They rode away, northward across the valley

and started up the twisting trail, neither looking back. Alec said, "That leaves three to go."

"Five as long as five are still alive. What's Colter really after, Alec? And these hardcases he's fetched in here?"

"I've asked myself that question a hundred times and I don't have an answer," Alec said. "Ain't made sense to me from the first." Sugar Sanders began pounding the triangle at the cook shack. "Let's put the feed bag on."

"Soon as I take care of my horse," Jim said, and as he walked away from Alec, he told himself that if he got the answer to his question, it would have to come from Ann Dunn.

CHAPTER VIII

Sugar Sanders showed as much enthusiasm as he had ever shown in his life when Jim walked into the cook shack with Alec. He shook hands, his melancholy face brightening. "By grab, you're looking fine, boy, damned fine."

"He's gonna fire Colter," Alec said. "He's chased the Mason boys already."

Sugar's face turned melancholy again. "Doc Finley just ordered a fresh batch of coffins," he said. "What size do you wear, son?"

"A .45," Jim answered, "but don't bury me yet.

79

I want to be mighty dead when you plant me. When I was a kid I remember Luke Dilly telling about that man they dug up after he'd been buried nine months. Luke said his hair had grown six inches and there were splinters under his fingernails. I had nightmares about that for weeks."

"Sit down," Sugar said as he poured coffee. "I'll tell Doc to be real careful before he lets 'em throw the clods on you."

"What the hell's the matter with you?" Alec said angrily. "All Jim needs is a little help."

"Reckon we can give it," Sugar said. "I don't know how big a batch of coffins Doc ordered. Sure hope it was three."

Jim winked at Alec. "Three years hasn't changed Sugar."

"Naw, and the next thirty won't neither." Alec grumbled. "The only thing that'll make us need them coffins is his biscuits. You wouldn't believe it, but they're getting tougher all the time."

"I eat 'em," Sugar said as if that settled the argument. "My stummick is real finicky, too."

"Finicky," Alec howled. "How 'bout the time we got lost when we was hunting and ran out o' grub. You couldn't find nothing but three horseshoes, so you fried 'em and et 'em. Finicky, hell."

Jim laughed. "It's good to be home," he said. "I didn't know how good. Just like it used to be, only when Luke Dilly and the old crew was here, everybody was firing at Sugar."

"Aw, he could handle all of us," Alec said. "If he couldn't, all he had to do was pour us another cup o' coffee, and it'd take the lining right off our tongues so we couldn't talk." He scratched the back of his neck, his face turning grave. "I just thought o' something, Jim. This is the first time we've joshed this way since Colter showed up. You don't feel like hooraying each other when you have to sit and look at that bastard's purty face."

"Naw, you sure don't," Sugar grunted. "My own grub don't even taste good no more."

They ate in silence after that, a somber mood falling upon all of them. Jim had some idea of the way it had been on the Box D. Probably Lennie Nolan was glad to live by himself up there on the divide in the line cabin. But why had they stayed, Alec and Sugar and Lennie? Why hadn't they gone with Luke Dilly and the rest of the old crew? There was only one answer that made any sense, loyalty to the Box D, and perhaps the hope that if Jim returned, life would be the way it had been when Sherm Dunn was alive, and Luke Dilly rodded the spread.

When they were done eating, Jim got up from the bench beside the long table and walking to the door, rolled a smoke. It was very still, with hardly a breath of wind to stir the leaves in the cottonwoods, and even with the sun shining from a clear sky, there was a sharp bite in the air. It would snow before long up there on the divide.

But how could a man do the work that must be done on a ranch if he had to fight, if his life was threatened every time he rode a narrow trail through the timber or down the side of a canyon? Or even when he walked along Cairo's Main Street at night.

"Where's Luke Dilly?" Jim asked.

"Grand Junction the last I heard," Alec said. "Buying and selling horses."

"And going broke at it," Sugar added.

"Would he come back if I sent for him?" Jim asked.

"Might," Alec said. "Sure was cut up about leaving."

"Did Dad fire him?"

"Well, he was fixing to give Luke another job . . ."

"Aw, quit your pussy footin'," Sugar cut in. "Sure he fired him. Needed a younger man, Sherm said."

Jim finished his cigarette and flipped it into the yard. Perhaps Luke had run out of steam, but he had the savvy. Jim wanted him back. Together they'd make a team. The old crew was scattered and could never be reassembled, but you could always hire riders.

A man could not reach back into time and bring it up to the present. It was a good thing he couldn't, Jim thought. You looked ahead, not back. If you were young, you dreamed your dreams. Jim and Ginny, here on the Box D. There'd be kids. Sure, there had to be. Half a dozen of them. Suddenly he caught himself. He had to see Ann Dunn. He couldn't keep putting it off. Maybe, like Ginny, he was afraid of her.

He turned to Alec. "When Colter rides in, let me know, but don't tell him I'm here."

Alec nodded. "You bet I will."

Jim left the cook shack, walking fast because he had to get this over with before he lost his nerve. He wasn't sure why he was afraid of the woman except that her record, to him at least, was completely black. She must be more than human to do all she had, some sort of witch. Or perhaps she had the power to hypnotize those who came in contact with her. He remembered the last time he had seen his father. Sherman Dunn looked as if he had found a new world which was inhabited only by him and Ann Delaney.

When Jim reached the cottonwoods, he could not force himself to go to the front door. He didn't know how to proceed. Should he knock before he went into his own house? Or should he just open the door and walk in? If he did and saw the woman, what should he do? What would he call her? Mrs. Dunn? Ann? Maybe, he thought sourly, she'd expect him to call her Mother.

Surrendering to his fears, he went around the house to the back, hoping to find Maggie

O'Boyle. He did. She was on the porch bending over a washtub, her arms in suds up to her elbows, entirely unaware that anyone was watching her. She was as big as ever, Jim thought, but her hair was grayer than he remembered.

"Hello, Maggie," he said.

She whirled with a great sweep of her skirt, the soap suds clinging to her arms. For just a moment she stood motionless, her mouth sagging open, so shocked she could not breath, then she came to all at once and plunged toward him, her arms outstretched, screaming, "Jim, Jim."

When she reached him, she threw her wet arms around him and hugged him so hard she squeezed the breath out of him. She kissed him on the cheek and hugged him again, and he had the feeling a great tent had dropped on him and completely enveloped him.

Finally she stepped back and looked at him affectionately. "Shame on you, Jim, for being gone so long. Have you had dinner? When did you get to town? How long have you been here? Have you seen Alec and Sugar?"

"A lot of questions. I had dinner . . ."

"All right, I can get the answers later." Grabbing an arm she led him into the kitchen. "Sit down. The coffee's hot and I've got a chocolate cake. Just like I used to make for you. I had a twitching in my left knee this morning when I got up. I didn't know what it was then, but I do now. The good Lord was telling me you were coming, and that's why I made the cake."

"Hold on, Maggie, hold on," he said. "You're like a big old ship coming into port with a hard wind in the sails . . ."

"A big old ship, is it?" she cried. "A big old ship . . ."

"I'm sorry." He patted her on the back. "I mean, a trim, neat little canoe caught in a rapids . . ."

"Oh, you and your blarney." She put her hands on her hips and looked at him. "I dunno, Jim, you talk just like you used to, but you don't look the same. I used to tell Sherm, I'd say, 'You won't know that boy when he gets back.' Why, I'd say to Sherm . . ."

"Maggie."

She was standing in the doorway of the dining room, looking at him, her lips slightly parted, her dark brown eyes bright with anticipation as if she knew who this stranger was before Maggie said a word. She was quite tall and slender, her height and slenderness accentuated by her close-fitting, black silk dress. Her hair, as black as her dress, was fluffed up above her forehead and pinned in a coil on top of her head.

"It's Jim, Ann," Maggie screamed as she always did when she was excited. "I told you he'd be back. Only this morning I had that twitching in my . . ."

"Oh Jim, I'm so glad you're here," Ann said.

85

He stood just inside the back door, not moving, not able to move. He had only heard this woman's voice, but he had mentally pictured her many times during the three years he'd been gone, and he had always been wrong.

Pretty was not the word to describe her. Handsome was better. Her features were far from perfect: her nose was too pointed, her chin a trifle sharp, her mouth much too long, but it was not her shortcomings that he noticed. There was something else that was hard to name, perhaps a radiance that reached out from her to touch him across this long room.

She walked to him, her eyes not leaving his, her lips still parted and smiling, and he could not help noticing her high-shouldered, high-breasted carriage, the grace with which she moved. Not with the careful fastidiousness of the good ladies of Cairo who were afraid some man on the street might realize they were women. Or the hip-flouncing walk of a floozy. It was somewhere between, as if she were a good woman, but still proud of the fact that she was a woman and wanted him to know it.

She put her hands on his arms and leaning forward, kissed him on the lips. She said, "You resemble Sherman a great deal, Jim. I think when he was your age, he must have looked exactly like you."

"Maggie used to tell me that," he said.

"That's just what I did," Maggie said. "The first time I ever saw Sherm was when they was laying out the Cairo townsite and he was standing behind one of them surveying rigs . . ."

"Maggie," Ann broke in, "I'm going to take Jim upstairs. We have a great deal to talk about."

"Upstairs?" he asked, surprised. "Why go upstairs to talk in a bedroom when we . . ."

"We made some changes up there, Jim. I want to show them to you."

"I was just going to cut him a piece of that chocolate cake I made this morning," Maggie said. "I was telling him about the twitch in my . . ."

"Bring cake and coffee," Ann said. "For both of us."

She took Jim's arm and guided him across the kitchen, leaving Maggie staring after them helplessly. She said, half to herself, "I've got a washing started, but reckon it ain't important."

Jim thought of a dozen things he could say, mean, knifing words that would tell Ann what he thought of her, but he said none of them. He had some hint of what had happened to his father. He had simply been carried away, his will a jelly-like thing that had given no resistance to her.

They went through the dining room. New furniture, he saw. A heavy-legged oak table and six chairs and a china cabinet against the wall. Through the front room that used to be littered with papers and catalogs and tally books and maybe even an old saddle or two. Now there was none of that. New furniture here, too. An orange-colored love seat. Rocking chairs. A dark blue Brussels carpet, so thick under foot that it smothered the sound of his boots on the floor. A dainty mahogany center table with legs that curved out and in and out again.

"We put new paper on the walls up here," Ann said as they climbed the stairs. "New carpet on the stairs and hall, too. But this is the biggest thing we did and one that made me very happy." She swung him around the white oak newel post at the top of the stairs and motioned toward what had been the front bedroom. "It's mine, Jim, my private parlor where I can shut the door and read or sew or do anything I want to."

He went in. New wallpaper, light and bright, red roses against a silver background. White lace curtains at the windows. A divan. Two rocking chairs. A sewing machine set against the wall. Several rag rugs on the floor. A small walnut stand in the centre of the room, the bottom of each leg a brass claw clutching a clear, glass ball.

He looked around, gripped by the strange feeling that he was having a weird dream, and in spite of all he could do, he could not wake up. This was home. But it wasn't home. Only the smoke blackened fireplace at one end of the room seemed natural. He looked at her and shook his head and she laughed.

"I know, Jim," she said. "I know exactly how you feel. It's all changed. If you don't like it . . ." She stopped, and for the first time, she seemed uncertain of herself. "I mean, we can change it back if you don't like it. We can't tear the wallpaper off, but we can make it into a bedroom again."

"No," he said.

She crossed the room to a rocking chair, and picking up a pillowcase she had been embroidering, sat down. "I hoped you would like it because I do." She motioned to a chair. "Won't you sit down, Jim?"

He took the chair, feeling oversize and awkward, and entirely out of place in this room which was so completely feminine. He put his hands on his knees and studied them, the big knuckles and tufts of reddish-brown hair on their backs. This was the time to tell her he hated her and he was going to fire her foreman and his crew and she could get to hell off the Box D.

He opened his mouth, but before a word came out, she said, "You hate me, don't you, Jim?"

He closed his mouth and swallowed. He watched her tighten the embroidery hoop, watched her needle take its little bite and her arm come up and pull the pink thread taut, and then do it all over again. Finally he said, "I've got reason to."

"Most people who get to know me learn to like me," she said. "And I certainly don't agree that you have any reason to hate me. It's true I'm responsible for your leaving home, but answer one question. Would you have been better off if you had stayed here?"

He thought of the past three years, how he'd wanted to drink and had whipped it. Ginny was always in his mind, and he blamed himself and his weakness for liquor for losing her. He thought of the hard work he had done, just another man in the saddle, making thirty a month and found, and sometimes when he couldn't get a riding job, how he'd taken anything he could get, or ridden the grub line. It had been hell in more ways than one.

But what if she had never come to the Box D and if he had stayed here? He'd have gone on just like he had, drinking and gambling and fighting. He'd have wound up another Monte Smith. No good. Just no damn good. A bar fly. Maybe he'd have been shot. Or gone to jail. His father would have thrown him out sooner or later. And he would have lost Ginny. For good.

He got up, jamming his hands into his pockets. "You're smart, ma'am, mighty smart. Of course I'm better off for what I've gone through. Like being purified in hell. Now I aim to fight for what's mine."

She looked up, startled. "Why, Jim, you don't have to fight. The ranch is yours." She started sewing again, and then said tentatively, "I would like to live here, but if you want me to leave, I will."

He walked around the room, seized by an inner turmoil that was new to him. Sure he wanted her off the Box D. Why, she could shoot him in the back just as Frank Castleman had tried to do. He wheeled and looked at her, at the glistening black-haired top of her head, and he wondered if he was wrong. Maybe she had nothing to do with the shooting last night.

"Why do you want to stay?" he asked.

"Because I've been happy here," she said simply. "I loved your father, Jim. He was almost twice my age, but I loved him. You see, he gave me the first real peace and security I ever knew."

She rose and dropping the pillowcase onto the chair, walked to him and gripped his arms, her face quite close to his. "This is the only home I can remember. I was grateful, so I did all I could to make Sherm happy. And I know I did. He told me many times that I did. He said I brought color to this house where there had been none. He said I made it alive. He used to sit here and look at me while I read or sewed. I'd ask him if there was anything I could do for him, and he'd say, 'No, I just want to look at you.' "

She put her arms around Jim and held him hard, her head against his chest. She said softly, "I've been looking forward to your being here. We need you, Jim. All of us. I'll do anything for you.

Anything you want if you'll let me stay."

The front door banged open and Alec called, "Jim."

He shoved her away from him and ran to the head of the stairs. "What is it, Alec?"

"Colter and Severe just rode in."

"I'm coming," Jim said.

Ann was behind him. She caught his arm. "What are you going to do?" she cried.

"Fire your man Colter," he said, and broke away from her and started down the stairs.

"Don't go, Jim," she screamed. "Don't go out there. They'll kill you."

He stopped halfway to the bottom and looked up at her. He asked, "Or are you afraid I'll kill him?"

He went on, almost running into Maggie at the foot of the stairs. She was holding a tray with two dainty cups in dainty saucers, a coffeepot, and a chocolate cake. "Jim, I've got your . . ."

He jerked his head at Alec. "We'll go through the back," and ran past Maggie. He stopped on the porch, standing with his back to the wall so he could not be seen, but he could see across the yard. Two men were walking to the bunkhouse, a large one and a very small one. The smaller, Jim told himself, would be the more dangerous of the two.

"Got a gun?"

"No hand gun," Alec answered. "I've got a Winchester, though."

"Where is it?"

"In the bunkhouse."

"Can you get at it?"

"Sure. It's leaning against the wall."

"You go in and sit down so you can reach it handy. Don't tell 'em I'm here. I'll give you thirty seconds, then I'll show up. Grab that rifle and hold it on Severe. Savvy?"

Alec's gaze touched Jim's face briefly. Jim read the fear that gripped him, fear that ran clear down into the bottom of his belly and twisted his insides into a knot. Jim knew how it was because he had felt that way a few times in his life. A scared man was poor backing, but it was all he had.

"Sure, Jim," Alec said, and started toward the bunkhouse.

Jim drew his gun, checked it carefully and slipped it back into the holster so it rode easily there, and then he followed Alec.

CHAPTER IX

Bud Colter found the Monument Rock range in better shape than he had expected. He would leave the young steers up here for a few days, he decided, and without discussing the matter with Toy Severe, headed back toward the Box D. By this time the news of Jim Dunn's death should have reached the ranch. He wanted to see how Alec Torrin and Sugar Sanders and Maggie took it, but even more than that, he wanted to see Ann.

There would be no putting him off now. He'd been patient. Sure, he understood her feelings. Mustn't offend Judge Riddle and Doc Finley and the rest of Sherm Dunn's friends by a quick marriage. Better wait until the property was all in Ann's name. Well, nobody should be offended after six months. As for the property, there could be no question now.

So he kept his horse at a fast pace, saying nothing to Severe who rode beside him. They dropped down into Ouray Valley three miles below the ranch and turned upstream toward it, passing the old Castleman house which had not been occupied since Sherm Dunn had bought the place from the bank. Colter rode with his head down, going over in his mind what he would say to Ann, so completely oblivious to what was happening around him that he was unaware Crip Lannigen rode ahead of them.

"Didn't figure Crip would get back till evening," Severe said.

Colter glanced up, jarred back into the present. Lannigen had pulled up and was waiting for them. When Colter drew abreast, Lannigen swung his horse around, saying, "They was needing salt up there all right. Should have taken some up last week."

It occurred to Colter that there was a possibility no one had brought the news of Dunn's death to the ranch. He couldn't go on waiting. If he didn't watch himself, he'd go to the house to see Ann and blurt out that Dunn was dead, then she'd want to know what had happened and how he had heard.

"Crip, take a sashay into town and pick up the mail," Colter said.

Lannigen looked at him sourly. He had been in the saddle all day and he didn't welcome the extra miles to town and back. He opened his mouth to argue, but Severe shook his head at him, and he caught the crankiness that was in Colter's face. He said, "All right, Bud," and angled across the valley toward the road that the Castlemans had used years ago. It was washed out in several places where it looped up the north mesa hill, but it was still possible for a horse to follow it to the top.

Colter watched him until he disappeared over the rim. Lannigen would be back by sundown, and he'd hear the instant he stopped on Cairo's Main Street. Colter felt his cheek. Better shave, he decided, before he went in to see Ann. If the news hadn't got here, there was no hurry. Well, he'd know as soon as he saw Alec Torrin, if Torrin was still around. In any case, the Mason boys would know.

But when Colter reached the Box D, Torrin was

not in sight. The loaded wheelbarrow was still in the corral. Colter swore, then decided Torrin had pulled out the instant he'd heard. He dismounted, loosened the cinch, and let his horse drink. Suddenly he realized the Masons weren't working with the saddle horses.

"Where do you suppose Ash and Del are?" he asked.

"Dunno," Severe said. "They sure ain't in sight."

They turned their mounts into the corrals and walked across the yard to the bunkhouse. The first thing Colter noticed was that Torrin's things were still there, including his Winchester which he would never go off and leave. So Torrin wasn't gone. That meant he hadn't heard. Then Ann hadn't, either.

Colter sat down on his bunk and rolled a smoke. It was a good thing he'd thought to send Lannigen to town. But why hadn't Judge Riddle or Hank Watrous brought the news to the ranch? Jim Dunn would be buried out here beside his father and mother. Ann would naturally be the first they'd notify.

Slowly Colter was forced to admit the possibility that Castleman had failed. But the shots had been fired! Colter had heard them. Moreover, he knew Castleman was a good marksman with a rifle. If he had missed, then all of Colter's planning was wasted.

Dunn would come out here and take over the

management of the Box D. But that meant more waiting, and Colter, whose nerves had been taut all day, knew he was not capable of much more waiting. Something had to give. That was when Alec Torrin walked into the bunkhouse.

Colter got up. He asked, "Alec, why didn't you finish the job I gave you?"

Torrin backed away, thoroughly cowed as he always was. "I got tired," he said. "I went into the house to see Maggie." He circled, facing Colter, and almost stepped on Severe's toes before he reached his own bunk. "I ain't as good a man as I used to be, Bud. You keep forgetting that."

"Maybe you never were any good," Colter said. "Well, I've had enough of this. You ain't worth your beans and you haven't been since I came here. Now pack up and git. You're fired."

"You've got that wrong, Colter," a man said from the doorway. "You're the one that's fired."

Colter wheeled. A stranger stood there, a big man, well-built, with good hands and heavy wrists and wide shoulders. But it was his eyes that drew and held Colter's attention, gray eyes that were fixed on him, utterly cold and merciless. Behind Colter Alec Torrin said, "This is Jim Dunn, Bud. I told you things would be different when he got back."

Colter knew who the stranger was before Torrin said that. There was a faint resemblance to old Sherm, the bold chin and the same strong, angular lines to his face. For a horrible moment Colter pictured in his mind a scene he would never entirely forget, of Sherm Dunn pitching off that narrow trail into Elk Canyon, of his body falling end over end, and finally coming to rest at the bottom with the flood of dirt and rocks following.

Colter lowered his eyes under Dunn's hard gaze. He wondered if he knew about his father. Or suspected. Sure he did. He must. He stood there in the doorway, his big-boned body almost filling it, waiting. He was an executioner, Colter thought wildly, come back after all these months. Colter could do nothing but go for his gun and Jim Dunn would kill him.

The moment of panic passed. Toy Severe was within a few feet of him. This was what he had brought the gunman to the Box D for. Colter said, "I don't believe this hardcase is Dunn." He turned to Severe. "How do you figure it, Toy?"

Colter intended to throw the play to the gunman, but Severe was having none of it. He said, "I ain't in this game, Bud. Alec's got me discommoded."

A quarter turn of the head showed Colter what the gunman meant. Torrin held his cocked Winchester on Severe. He wasn't cowed now. He said, "This is what I've been waiting for, Bud. I'm just hoping this snaky son goes for his gun."

From the doorway Dunn said, "Get moving, Colter. If you've got anything here you want, pack it up and get out. The Mason boys didn't take anything. They said to tell you they'd be in Cairo."

So that was it. Colter looked at Dunn, measuring him, and deciding there was only one way he could play it. A gamble, sure, but better than crawling out on his belly. He said, "I don't believe you're Jim Dunn. I figure you're some drifter Torrin got hold of to pretend he was Dunn because there's a chance of getting a damned fine ranch. If you expect me to take your word . . ."

"I don't give a damn if you take my word or not," Dunn said. "Just get out of here and stay off the Box D. That's all I ask."

"You're the one that's getting off," Colter said. "No saddle bum's riding in and throwing me off a spread I've been rodding for almost three years. If it comes to throwing, I'll do it."

He started toward the door. Dunn did not step aside or back up. A lesser man would have done one or the other. Colter had learned years ago that it was an effective maneuver. He knew he was impressive-looking; he had size and strength to go with it, and when he moved directly upon a man who was standing against him, that man invariably moved aside.

The trouble this time was it didn't work. Jim Dunn simply stood there. When Colter realized he wasn't going to move, he hesitated, and that was his undoing. Dunn came alive in a burst of action

99

much like a giant spring that has been wound too tightly and suddenly explodes into a whirring, snarling burst of violence. Dunn's left fist lashed out. Colter threw up his guard instinctively and ducked. The left did not come through, but the right did, catching Colter squarely on the side of the head and knocking him sprawling.

Colter jumped up and lunged at Dunn, both fists swinging. He was a good man in a fight and he seldom lost. He obeyed no rules. Head butting, elbows, knees, boots: anything went if the opportunity came. Suddenly he was glad it had worked this way. If there ever was a man he wanted to beat down into the dirt and use his boots on, it was Jim Dunn.

But he didn't land either fist. He was on his back, his head ringing, looking up at Dunn, and he heard Dunn's voice come to him from a great distance, "Get up, you son of a bitch. Get up and fight."

He did, but this time with caution, both fists cocked in front of him. They circled, facing each other, and he felt blood drip from his nose. He threw out a tentative right, but Dunn wouldn't open up. "You looked for a minute like a real fighting man, Bud," Torrin taunted. "Down there on the floor." He wasn't to be goaded into rushing Dunn again, so they circled like two cagey roosters, then when he least expected it, Dunn was on him, using both fists to his body.

Colter took those blows for a chance at Dunn's face. He threw his right, short and wicked, but it was a little high, too high for a knockdown. Dunn's head rocked back, and Colter fell forward, got him by the waist and wrestled him to the floor. This was Colter's kind of fighting. They went over and over again, Colter using his fists and knees, and once he brought his head squarely down on Dunn's mouth, cutting a lip and bringing a rush of blood.

They crashed into the stove and knocked it over. The stovepipe fell to the floor with a terrific clatter and soot rushed out in a plague of black dust. They hit the wall and bounced off. They rolled over again, and as they turned, Dunn got in two hard blows to Colter's chin. They struck the rickety bureau at the far end of the room and knocked it over.

Dunn was clear when the bureau fell, but a corner caught Colter's ankle, sending waves of pain rocketing up his leg. He had a horrible moment of fear, thinking it was broken or sprained, and he would have lain there if Dunn hadn't said, "You're yellow, Colter, yellow all the way through."

Dunn was on his feet and backing away, wiping his face with his sleeve and smearing the soot from ear to ear until he was more black than white. Slowly Colter got to his hands and knees, watching Dunn, blood drooling from his nose and spreading across his upper lip. He tasted it, drew in a long breath, and knew he was licked.

But he tried. He got to his feet, not sure his injured ankle would hold him. It did, and then the room started to tip and whirl, and he had the terrifying experience of seeing two Jim Dunns in front of him, twins, both equally big. He stumbled toward one of them, not sure he had picked the right one; he started an uppercut from the top of his boots that missed completely and swung him off balance.

Dunn took one step forward and caught him flush on the jaw. Colter's knees buckled and he was down again, not completely out but lacking both the power and the will to get back on his feet and keep fighting.

"Go saddle up your horses, Severe," Jim said. "Fetch 'em here. We'll tie this bastard in the saddle if we have to. You go with him, Alec. Let him keep his gun. I hope he pulls it. Then you can kill him."

"I'll pull it later," Severe said. "Bud won't forget this. Neither will I."

Dunn spit out a mouthful of blood. He said, "If you've got any sense, Severe, you'll leave the country. I know you're wanted in Texas."

Severe left the bunkhouse, saying nothing more. Colter heard this, but he lay there, not moving, not even wanting to move. Blood dribbled from his nose and spread into his mouth. He swallowed and almost gagged. He put a hand against the floor and pushed. No use.

He had a strange feeling that his mind was alive, but his body was dead. He had lost Ann. He had lost the Box D. Everything he had worked and waited and schemed for, all gone. Dunn, standing by the door, hideously ugly with his swollen lip and blood-and-soot smeared face, seemed to be justice personified come back to punish him for the murder of Sherman Dunn.

Now, with the minutes dragging out, Bud Colter was aware of the certainty of one thing; he would kill Jim Dunn or Dunn would kill him. His gun was still in his holster. He could move his right hand. If he did, he would die, for that was what Dunn was waiting for. There would be a later time, a better time.

In all his life Bud Colter had never hated a man as much as he hated Jim Dunn. He understood how Frank Castleman felt, but Castleman was a fool. Colter wasn't. There would be a way. It meant more waiting. That was all.

Severe was in front of the bunkhouse with the horses. Dunn said, "Get up."

Colter struggled to his feet, his mind racing on ahead of his battered body. *Kill him,* it said. *Kill him.* But his body did not obey. He reached the front door and leaned against the casing, his head tipping forward. Dunn, backing into the yard, called impatiently, "Come on, come on."

He stumbled to his sorrel and gripped the horn; he lifted one foot to the stirrup and that was all he could do. Dunn gave him a boost into the saddle and he almost fell on over the horse on the other side, but his left hand, still gripping the horn, steadied him.

"Get out of the country," Dunn said. "You and your whole damned bunch. If you don't, Colter, I'll kill you. And I'll wire the Texas Rangers that Severe is here if I ever see him again."

Severe was already riding out of the yard. Colter followed, hanging tenaciously to the saddle horn, while waves of pain struck at him continuously. They crossed the valley and climbed the steep hill to the north, then Severe stopped.

"*Adios*, Bud," he said. "I've got to start riding."

"Not as long as Dunn's alive." Colter had taken the beating, but Alec Torrin had held a Winchester on Severe and made him saddle the horses. Severe was never one to forget an injury. Knowing that, Colter added, "Hide out somewhere. Give me a day to get over this. Then we'll get Dunn and Torrin both."

He saw desire grow in the gunman's pinched, wicked little face until it overshadowed his natural caution. "All right," he said. "I'll be at Monument Rock."

Severe struck off to the west. He'd make out. There was an old cabin at the foot of Monument Rock that had been built years ago by a trapper or prospector. It was still tight, and equipped with blankets and a stove and several days' supply of food. Sherm Dunn had kept it that way in case some of his men were caught in a storm, and Colter had continued the practice. Now it would be used for something else. All five of them could hole up there for a few days if necessary.

Colter rode on toward town, still holding to the saddle horn. He had never taken a beating like this, but worse than that was his fear that he knew what Ann would do, now that Dunn was back. She would have no more use for Bud Colter. Or so she was thinking. But there would come a day when she'd need him again. She'd find that out.

So he rode, with each thumping ache of his head fostering the hate he felt for Jim Dunn.

CHAPTER X

Jim did not move from where he stood in front of the bunkhouse until Colter and Severe reached the north mesa hill and started to climb. He heard Alec say, "You handled him. Man, man, you sure handled him. I guess we've seen the last of them."

But they hadn't. Colter was like Frank Castleman. Jim had beaten him half to death, but nothing had changed. Castleman would go on hating him and waiting for a chance to kill him.

Possibly Severe had been scared out of the country. But not Bud Colter. He'd find the Masons in town. Crip Lannigen was still around. So there would be four of them at least.

"Clean up the bunkhouse," Jim said thickly, his battered lip feeling as big as a flapjack.

He walked to the horse trough and sloshed water over his face, touching his mouth tenderly; he bent and scrubbed, for the soot clung to him with stubborn tenacity. He started for the house, remembering with a sense of shame how Ann had affected him. But not again, not after seeing Bud Colter, and fighting with him. Colter was her man. He must be, for she had brought him to the Box D.

He went in through the back door. Maggie straightened from stoking up the kitchen range; she looked at him and cried, "Jim, what happened?"

"I fired Colter and Severe." He sat down at the table. "Soak a rag in cold water. He butted me on the mouth like a damned billy goat."

She took a rag to the back porch, worked the pump handle until the water came cold, soaked the rag and wrung it out, then brought it to him. He said, "Sit down, Maggie. I want to know some things about his woman upstairs," and held the wadded-up rag against his mouth.

Maggie shook her head at him. "Now Jim boy, you've got no call to . . ."

He removed the rag from his mouth. "I've got

106

plenty of call. I'm fighting for my life. And the Box D. I don't trust her, and we'll have trouble with Colter till he's dead. I've got a right to know where she came from and how Colter got here and why they hate Dad in town."

He put the rag back to his mouth and waited. Maggie was plainly distressed. She walked to the stove, saying, "The coffee's hot and . . ."

"No," he said from behind the rag.

She looked out the window down the long trough of the valley with its haystacks, turned brown by rain and sun, and then she rubbed her big face with both hands. She said, "Jim, I felt like you do when Ann first came and when she asked Sherm to fire Luke. Then she fetched Colter in and I hated her." She sighed. "I thought the Box D would go to pot and she'd make Sherm spend a lot of money on her, but I was wrong. They fixed the upstairs to suit her and that was all she asked for. She was a good wife. I don't care what they think or say in Cairo. She was a good wife and she made him happy."

"You loved Dad," Jim said. "I always figured he'd marry you some day."

She smiled briefly. "Sure I loved him. I was jealous when he brought Ann here, but I got over it. I was just a housekeeper to him." She looked down at her red, work-roughened hands. "No use fooling myself. I'm a plow horse and Ann's a hotblood mare. I couldn't have done for Sherm

107

what she did. Loving wasn't enough. He needed something else."

"What about the way the people in town feel toward him?"

"I don't know," she said wearily. "I don't think they ever loved him. Not many people did. He was a hard man to love. It was worse after Ann came. He took her to church, but the women wouldn't have anything to do with her. Then he tried to force men into making their wives take her into one of their clubs. You know that wouldn't work. He got mad and kept making things worse."

Jim nodded, understanding how that would be. His father had always been bullheaded, but the women of Cairo would be too tough even for him to whip. He rose and laid the wet rag on the table. "I guess I'd better go up and talk to her."

"Be good to her, Jim," Maggie said. "She took Sherm's death awfully hard."

He thought about that as he climbed the stairs. If she had fooled Maggie, she was a good actress, for Maggie was hard to fool. Ann came to the door of her parlor before he reached it; she gripped both of his arms and looked up at him, and he saw she had been crying.

"I was frightened," she said. "I know what Bud's like, and that Severe is a snake. Then I saw them ride away and I knew you were all right."

When he was away from her, he could hate her, but he could not when he was with her. He had only to look at her to understand the fire she had built in his father. He said, "Sit down, I've got some questions to ask."

"You're hurt." Gently she touched his bruised mouth. "Isn't there something I can do?"

"No. I want you to tell me how Dad met you and how Colter got here."

She sat down in her rocking chair and folded her hands in her lap. He stood there looking at her, and he could not help admiring her calm serenity and self-assurance. If she was guilty of any crime, or if she had any knowledge of a crime, she gave no indication of it.

"It's natural that you'd want to know," she said. "You'll have to sit down, too. I can't talk when you're standing up."

So he sat down, feeling as awkward as he had before and wishing they were downstairs. He put his hands on his knees and sat with his shoulders hunched forward, wondering if his lip looked as big to her as it felt to him.

He said, "Go ahead."

"First you should know that for years I was an entertainer in saloons and dance halls and opera houses. I've traveled all over Texas and New Mexico and even west to California. Usually I was with a group. For awhile Colter was my manager, I guess he's done almost everything at one time or another, including ranching. He had a big spread in New Mexico which he inherited from his father, but he lost it in the panic of '93."

She looked directly at Jim, apparently feeling no shame or embarrassment because of her past. He asked, "Did Dad know how you'd made your living?"

"Yes, but that didn't bother him. Well, Colter arranged for me to meet Sherm. I don't know exactly how they had met, but Sherm was in Pueblo, and Colter passed himself off as a rancher who had sold out and was looking for another location. I was in Trinidad in a show. Colter wired for me to come to Pueblo. I did, and we made a deal that if I married Sherm, I'd get Colter a good job. I kept my part of the bargain."

"What about Luke Dilly?"

"I'm to blame for his being fired," she said frankly. "I'm not sorry. He was an old man. He couldn't get around like a foreman should on a big place like this, so Sherm had to do things that Dilly should have done. When evening came, he was always tired. I needed a husband, Jim, and I had every intention of being a good wife. I was, after Colter came. I suppose you liked Dilly and you think it was wrong to let him go, but I think I did right." She leaned forward. "Jim, please try to understand this. For two and a half years I made Sherm happy. I didn't try to do anything else. It was all I wanted to do."

He was embarrassed by her frankness. He rolled a cigarette, his eyes on the paper and tobacco in front of him. "What's Colter to you?"

"Nothing," she said. "I know there's been gossip in town because it's common knowledge I brought him here, but gossip is a cheap and wicked thing, and Cairo is full of cheap and wicked women. Sherm and I were not really happy until I convinced him that I wanted no part of Cairo's social life. I was satisfied just to be with him."

He reached into his vest pocket for a match. "They hate Dad in town. They claim he used the bank to steal people's land."

"And I suppose they blame me for that," she said hotly. "It isn't true. Times had been hard for the last two years. A bank is in business to loan money. What can it do when the borrowers can't pay the interest? Just one of two things. Be generous and give more time and eventually go broke. Or take the land to protect the bank. That was what Sherm did. He said a solvent bank was more important to a community than carrying men like Hank Watrous who would be failures no matter what they did."

He got up and walked to a window. A wind had sprung up and was making a faint cry around the eaves, and somewhere in the back of the house a loose window rattled. He would have to find it and fix it, he thought absently. He put his cigarette out. Smoking was no pleasure with his cut lip. He said, "Colter murdered Dad, didn't he?"

For a moment she was too stunned to answer.

Then she rose and came to him. "Why do you ask that? Is it some more of the gossip you've heard?"

He shook his head. "I just added things up. Dad was too good a rider and Sundown is too good a horse to have an accident like that."

"And you think I had something to do with it. Well, you're wrong. I had every reason to want Sherm to live."

"What's Colter got in his head for this tough crew he hired? Men like Toy Severe don't make a habit of riding for thirty a month and beans."

"I don't know. I never asked him. He hired them and Sherm didn't object as long as they did their work."

"I was shot at last night in Cairo," he said. "Judge Riddle told me that if I died, or failed to run the Box D to his satisfaction, you'd inherit everything."

She stared at him, her face very pale. Then she began to tremble, the corners of her mouth quivering. "You do hate me . . ." she whispered. "You think I'm a monster who would . . ." She couldn't go on. She motioned toward the door. "You'd better leave, Jim."

He left, ashamed as he had never been ashamed of anything in his life, yet all the circumstances pointed to her guilt, or so it seemed to him. Any jury whose members did not know her personally would have declared her guilty, but not if they knew her, and that was what made him ashamed.

Alec Torrin was on her side. And Maggie who was with her every day. They must be right, he thought. They must be. Still, he was not sure. He wondered if he would ever be.

Before he reached the front door Maggie called, "Jim." He turned, waiting while she crossed the room to him. She gave him a sharp, scrutinizing look, then she said, "You have been hard on her, ain't you?"

He said, "Don't rawhide me, Maggie."

She sighed. "Jim boy, there's enough trouble for all of us without fighting with her. She deserves better. You'll eat with us, won't you? It's been right lonesome for her since Sherm died, with nobody but me for company."

"I wouldn't be good company."

"You won't sleep in the bunkhouse, anyhow. Your old room's ready for you. I made it up fresh just now."

He started to say he belonged in the bunkhouse, then he thought it was no way to start if the Box D was going to be his. Besides, he didn't want Ann to think she had driven him out of his own bed. A small victory, but not one he wanted her to have. He said, "Sure, Maggie. I'll sleep up there."

He went out into the wind, tugging his hatbrim down so the hat sat tightly on his head. The sun was far down to the west, throwing its long scarlet banners across the horizon. Alec came out of the bunkhouse and fell into step with him. He said, "I got it cleaned up. You reckon Colter and his bunch will be back to pick up their stuff?"

"Sure they will." They kept pace for awhile, then Jim said, "I'm going up to the divide in the morning. I want you to go to town and wire Luke in Grand Junction. Tell him to come on the run and fetch a crew if he can find one. Take that livery horse back to Hofferd when you go."

"Sure," Alec said.

They walked on past the barn until they reached the pasture fence. Alec said, "I want to know what you think Colter will do. He might get real ornery if he comes back."

"You mean he might burn us out?" Jim shook his head. "I don't think so. It's my guess he's after the Box D. He's going to be mighty sure he hasn't got a chance at it before he gets any notion about burning us out."

He opened the gate into the pasture and shut it, Alec remaining outside. Jim called to Sundown, and the big bay came to him, whinnying, his ears tipped forward. He had belonged to Sherman Dunn, but Jim had been the only one who had ridden him up until the time he had left. If he had not parted from his father in the manner he had, he would have tried to trade for or buy the gelding, but neither of them had been in a mood to talk horse trade.

It was just as well, he thought, as he patted Sundown's neck. There had been a time in La Junta when he couldn't get work and had sold his horse. Sundown nuzzled him, and Alec called, "He's trying to kiss you, Jim. He sure ain't forgot."

"Naw, he'd never forget," Jim said. "I sure wish he could talk."

"So do I," Alec said. "Nobody's rode him since the day they brought Sherm in. Colter got on him once and Sundown piled him. Colter's a good rider, too."

Jim ran a hand along the horse's back. "I wish he'd killed him."

"That's a funny thing." Alec cuffed back his hat and scratched his head as if he wasn't sure he believed what he'd seen. "That horse did try to kill him. Yes sir, he tried, and he'd have done it if the Mason boys hadn't been there. After that Colter wouldn't even get into the pasture with Sundown."

Jim grinned as he let himself back through the gate. "He's a smart horse, Alec. I guess that don't leave much doubt about what Colter did."

"I've sure thought a lot about it," Alec said, "but damn it, you can't take that kind of evidence into court."

"No," Jim said, "but it satisfies me."

He ate supper in the cook shack, or tried to, but his lip bothered him. He rolled and lighted a cigarette. It still didn't taste good, and he put it out. He said, "Fill a sack with grub, Sugar. I'll take it up to Lennie in the morning."

He went out into the dusk, sore in a dozen places where he had been bruised by Colter's fists or had been thrown against the wall or stove during their wild melee on the floor. For a time he stood with his back against a cottonwood, old memories returning to him, some good, some bad. He tried to keep Ann Dunn out of his mind. He wanted to think of Ginny. Maybe he should ride into town and see her tonight, but he knew he couldn't. Bed was the place for him.

He walked slowly to the house, wondering if there could be anything in what Alec had said about Colter's coming back. Would he turn vengeful, knowing that whatever plans he'd had were ruined, and burn Box D to the ground?

That was the one thing he could not stand, Jim thought. Maybe he should stay here. Or try to hire some men in Cairo. Then he thought Colter wouldn't try anything yet, and with that thought was the knowledge that Ann Dunn was his best insurance.

When he went upstairs, Ann's parlor was dark, but as he turned toward his own room, he saw a crack of light under her bedroom door. He knocked, and she called at once, "Come in, Jim."

He opened the door to find her sitting in front of her mirror that hung on the wall near her bureau. Her long black hair hung down her back. She was brushing it with regular, sweeping strokes, and as he stood in the doorway looking at her, he could understand how his father had been so completely in love with her. Funny, he thought, how that notion always came to him when he was with her.

Ann turned her head and smiled at him, then turned back and went on brushing her hair. She said, "I knew you'd come home someday, Jim, and above all things I wanted to be friends with you. The trouble is you make it very difficult."

"I'm sorry," he said. "I want you to stay here."

"I have no intention of leaving," she said. "Not until the estate is settled anyhow, and that won't be for six months." She put her brush down and rose and faced him. "Would it help if I told you I have no idea why Colter hired the kind of crew he did, that if he killed Sherm, I had no knowledge of it, and as far as I'm concerned, I want nothing to do with him, and I have repaid everything I owe him."

She was wearing nothing but her nightgown that reached from her chin to her ankles, and although it fitted her with sack-like looseness, it did not detract from the high-shouldered, high-breasted way she carried herself that told him she was proud of her body.

Embarrassed, he felt his cheeks burn as he backed into the hall. He said, "Yes, I want to believe that."

"Wait, Jim." She crossed the room to him. "I want to be friends. I don't want to quarrel with you about Sherm's property. Or anything. I just

117

want to convince you that you shouldn't hate me. You know, he used to sit there in my parlor, smoking and looking out the window toward the north rim. He'd say, 'One of these days Jim will ride down that trail.' " She sighed. "I wish you had before he died."

"So do I," he said. "Good night."

He walked down the hall to his old room, and somehow he felt better. He could get along with her, for awhile at least. If she were guilty, she would play it out with Colter while they tried to get him out of the way. If she wasn't, well, that presented a variety of problems.

The simplest solution would be to marry Ginny and bring her out here to live, but that, he knew, would be the surest way of raising hell that he could think of.

Chapter XI

Bud Colter met Crip Lannigen on the bridge in Cairo. He said, "We're fired. No use going to the Box D."

"But I've got some stuff . . ."

"We'll get it tomorrow," Colter said. "We'll have the sheriff go out there with us."

Lannigen swung his horse around. "Who fired us?"

"Jim Dunn."

Lannigen was silent as he rode into town with Colter, but he kept glancing at the other man's face, and finally, just before they reached the hotel, Colter said, "All right, I suppose you've got to know. Jim Dunn was at the ranch when Toy and I rode in. He whipped me. He whipped the hell out of me." A moment later he reined up in front of the hotel and painfully dismounted, holding to the horn until a wave of nausea had passed. He said, "Take my horse down to Hofferd's stable. Then get me a new shirt in the Mercantile and bring it to me."

He went inside, reeling like a drunk. Right now he wanted only one thing, to get a room and lie flat on his back in a bed. So he signed the register, ignoring the clerk's stare, took the key and stumbled up the stairs. He stopped almost at the top, hanging to the banister while the building went into a spin like a boy's top.

A drummer, coming down to supper, asked, "Can I help you, friend?"

Colter went on, saying nothing. He got to his room and pushed the door open and spilling across the bed, lay there, his hat falling off and dropping to the floor. He was that way when Lannigen came in with his shirt.

Colter turned over on his back. "Run into Ash and Del?"

"No."

"They're in town. Go find 'em."

Lannigen went out, shutting the door behind him. With an effort, Colter got to his feet. He held to the head of the bed for a moment, then crossed to the bureau and poured water into the white bowl. He pulled off his soiled shirt and threw it across the room, then he made the mistake of looking into the mirror and almost fainted.

He shut his eyes and grabbed the top of the bureau. This was the first time in his life, or the first time he could remember when he had not found his face a thing of beauty to admire. All he could see were bruises and cuts and a great, hideous clot of blood clinging to his upper lip from his nose.

He dabbed water on his face. It felt as if he were pricking it with a thousand needles. He pried the clot of blood loose, carefully blotted his face dry with the towel, and went back to bed. He was lying there when Lannigen came in with the Mason brothers.

Lannigen lighted a lamp. Ash Mason took one look at Colter's face and whistled. "Say, that Sundown didn't kick you in the mug, did he?"

Colter sat up on the edge of the bed, gripping the sides with both hands. He said, "Don't get smart, Ash. I didn't notice you tackling Dunn, and there's two of you."

Ash got red in the face. "Hell, he had a gun on us before we even knowed he was there."

"All right, all right," Colter said. "Today he was a better man than I am. Maybe tomorrow he won't be. I aim to find out about that."

"Where's Toy?" Lannigen asked.

"At Monument Rock. Dunn knew Toy's wanted in Texas, so he decided to stay out of sight."

"Is he leaving the country?"

"Later, maybe. After we get square with that Dunn bastard."

Lannigen looked at the Mason brothers who nodded at him. He cleared his throat. He said uneasily, "Bud, we've been working for more'n two years, figuring on making ourselves rich according to you. Where is it?"

A few hours before Colter had told himself that with Jim Dunn out of the way, he had everything lined up. He'd marry Ann, she'd get old Sherm's property, and all he had to do was to figure out how to get rid of his tough crew. Now everything was changed. He needed all four of them, but it was like Toy Severe had said. So far all they'd had was the hole in the doughnut.

He looked at Lannigen, then at Ash Mason, and finally at Ash's brother Del. They were returning his stare, questioningly, almost challengingly. He could guess what was in their minds. They were looking at a man who had been whipped and fired, and any chance they had of stealing some of Box D's wealth was gone. It would take very little to make them saddle up and ride out of the

121

country. But he couldn't let them go. Not yet.

"It's right where it always was," he said. "When the sign's right, we'll grab it. The first chore is to get rid of Dunn, then we'll be back where we were."

"And how do we get rid of Dunn?" Ash Mason demanded. "From all I heard, I figured he'd be a no-good drunk, but he's about as salty as they come."

"We've guessed wrong about him," Colter agreed. "You boys had supper?"

"No," Del said.

"Go put the feed bag on," Colter said. "Then take a look into Rafferty's before you come up."

They hesitated, shuffling uncertainly. It was then Colter realized they had agreed to pull out, but the habit of obedience was strong in them and they left finally. He lay back on the bed, for the moment giving himself over to the luxury of sheer hatred and mentally picturing Jim Dunn lying in the dust with a bullet hole in his head.

Colter flexed his fingers; he opened and closed his hands. Stiff. He'd hit Dunn enough to bruise his knuckles. He'd be slow with a gun for a few days. Besides, he had a hunch Dunn would be fast. The idea of calling him into the yard and going for his gun wasn't a good one, not a good one at all. Colter was never one to take a gamble when the odds were against him. There had to be a better way.

He closed his eyes, putting his mind to work. He could still count on Ann. He could use Castleman, but not in the way he had planned. Probably the thing to do was to hide out at Monument Rock for a few days, then take advantage of the first opportunity to kill Dunn and wait for Ann to rehire him as a foreman. Tonight he would discredit Dunn here in town.

The big problem was to raise enough money to take care of his men. He didn't know how much they would expect. He had planned on getting enough money from Ann to pay them off, maybe three thousand apiece, but that wouldn't do. Now that he considered it in the cold realism of this moment, he knew he had been whistling in the dark anyhow. They would never have been satisfied with three thousand.

He had two possibilities. One was to gather a herd of Box D steers and sell them in the mining camps of the San Juan. There was still time if they didn't get a big October storm. They could round up three hundred head without much difficulty, and it would not be hard to locate a butcher who would take them and have them sold over the block before Hank Watrous caught up with them. If the boys were lucky, they might get sixty dollars a head. Divided four ways, that wouldn't be bad. He'd deal himself out. Once that he was back in the saddle on the Box D, he could take very good care of Bud Colter.

The other possibility was the bank. There should be at least forty thousand dollars in the safe. It might be more dangerous than taking their steers, but only for the few minutes they were actually in the bank and on their way out of town. In the long run it would be less dangerous.

The boys knew the country. Once across the Uncompahgre Plateau, they'd hit for the Utah line. There were hideouts in the Blue Mountains. After that, it would be a matter of staying out of circulation for a few months.

Well, he could decide this later. He had held off on the bank because it would go to Ann when the estate was settled, and eventually to him. Certainly a man was a fool to rob his own bank, but if it was the only way to get his crew off his neck, then that was what he'd do.

He got up and washed his face again, and found that the dizziness did not return. It was just that he hurt in so damned many places. He got into his new shirt and combed his hair, then sat down to wait. His mind went back to his own youth when he was Jim Dunn's age. He had owned a spread just about the size of the Box D, and he'd lost it because he'd been young and cocky.

Since then he'd never owned anything. He'd taken his chances on the owl hoot, but no more of that. It wasn't the smart way to live, Toy Severe had found that out, even if the others hadn't. He'd got into the show business, managing a bunch of girls, booking them through the Southwest and taking a share of their earnings. He'd tried his hand at con games of one sort or another, at promotion schemes which never paid off, and all the time he knew there was only one thing that would satisfy him, to own land again, to be big as Sherm Dunn had been here on the Uncompahgre.

So, when he had spotted Sherm Dunn in Pueblo as a ripe plum ready to be plucked, he'd sent for Ann. It had worked, the first deal of the kind that ever had worked for him. Ann had better remember, he thought. She'd better be damned sure she remembered.

Lannigen and the Masons came in. Colter got up. He asked, "Who's in Rafferty's?"

"The usual town crowd," Lannigen said. "Judge Riddle and Bill Royal and that bunch."

Colter nodded. "Crip, you'll stay here with me tonight. Ash and Del, you boys go to Castleman's place and take him to Monument Rock. Get him out of town without any fuss. Slug him if you have to. Blow out the lamp and shut the door. Make it look as if he'd taken a ride and just didn't come back. Crip and me will see you at Monument Rock about noon tomorrow."

"No dice," Ash said stubbornly. "I'm ready for the pay-off. Where is it?"

"As long as Jim Dunn's alive, there'll be no pay-off," Colter said. "The day he's in hell, there will be. If you boys don't like it, ride out of here tonight. You've been working for me for more'n two years. You've been comfortable and had good grub and you've been paid better'n average wages. You're wanted, somewhere or other, but you haven't had to worry because no law man would look for a wanted man on the payroll of a ranch like the Box D."

Colter jerked a thumb toward his chest. "You owe that to me. I haven't needed you before. I do now. All I've got to say is that you're a purty damned low, scurvy bunch of mavericks if you don't play this out."

They looked at each other, moving their feet around uneasily just as they had before they'd gone down to supper. They could not stand before him. He had a talent for leadership; there was none among them. Still, they had agreed to a showdown. He sensed that, for he had been whipped, and like the proverbial rats in the sinking ship, they wanted off.

"All right, I know what you're thinking," Colter said. "I took a licking today. Well, I'll never take another one. That's a promise. Once we get rid of Dunn, I'll be right back where I was."

"Then what?" Ash asked skeptically.

"Then we cut the melon."

"What melon?" Ash demanded. "That's the nub of this whole thing. We don't see no damned melon."

"The bank." It was Colter's ace and he knew this was the time to play it. "I figure it'll pay off ten thousand apiece."

That satisfied them. Lannigen lingered in the doorway, then he said, "Guess I'll get a drink and roll in."

"I'll go down with you," Colter said.

Near the door Colter stooped and picked up his hat. When he bent over, his head began to pound and he came close to falling forward. He straightened, grabbed the door casing, and held on to it until his head cleared. Lannigen was already in the hall. They went down the stairs together, Colter wondering what he'd have said if the Masons and Lannigen had told him they'd cut the melon tonight. There was nothing to keep them from busting the bank safe open and be on their way, and to hell with him and Toy Severe. But they hadn't.

He repressed a smile as he left the hotel with Lannigen, for he was remembering how the three of them had followed the groove of thinking he had laid out for them, all of which went to prove that some men are born to lead and some are born to follow. With any kind of luck he'd soon be wearing Sherm Dunn's boots when he walked down Cairo's Main Street.

Tonight, as on all weekday nights, Rafferty's was not crowded. There wasn't a farmer or cowboy in the lot until Colter came in with

Lannigen. Just townsmen: Judge Riddle, Doc Finley, Shep Hofferd, Bill Royal, and two or three more lined up along the bar talking. Doc Finley was up to his ears in a poker game with a couple of drummers, a tall pile of blue chips in front of him, a pleased expression on his round face that always seemed as innocent and pink-cheeked as a boy in his early teens.

"Whiskey," Colter said.

"The same," Lannigen said.

Rafferty set out a bottle and glasses, then he looked at Colter and whistled. "What happened to you, Bud?"

"Horse threw me."

"Thought you were a better rider than that," Rafferty said.

"So did I." Colter took his drink and felt the whiskey's welcome warmth work through him. Judge Riddle was on his right, Lannigen on his left, and Colter saw that Riddle had turned from Bill Royal and was staring at him. Colter said, "I guess you knew Jim Dunn was back."

"Yes, I knew," Riddle said.

Colter poured another drink. "That boy sure has an eye for women. I'd heard about him, but you never know when you just hear someone talking." He shook his head. "Well, its more'n talk. He got one look at his dad's widow and he didn't want me around no more. So I'm fired. Not that I blame him. Mrs. Dunn's a fine-looking woman." He took his drink and set the glass down. "No bunkhouse for young Dunn. No sir. He moves into his old room right next to where Mrs. Dunn sleeps. Mighty handy, seems to me."

Colter threw a coin down on the bar, and in the sudden, frosty silence the tinkle of silver against the mahogany was a great racket. "Well, Crip, let's roll in. I'm sleepy."

The silence did not break until they were outside and the bat wings swished shut behind them, then he grinned as he heard Rafferty explode, "That filthy-tongued bastard!" And Bill Royal, "How do you know he's wrong, Raff?"

Colter was still grinning when he went into his room and pulled off his boots. He could not admire his face tonight, but he could admire his brain. He dropped off to sleep at once, the smile lingering at the corners of his mouth.

Chapter XII

When Jim first woke, he was so stiff and bruised from his fight with Colter that he thought he couldn't get out of bed. He lay there for a time, finding some satisfaction in the certainty that if Colter was waking up now, he was worse off. Maybe he'd stay in bed all day. But it didn't make much difference whether Colter got up today or tomorrow. Regardless of the game he was playing, he would not rest until Jim Dunn was dead. Of that Jim was sure. First Castleman, now Colter. It was not a pleasant feeling.

Jim forced himself to get up and dress, finding that some of the stiffness left him when he began to move around. He opened the door carefully, not wanting to wake Ann, and went downstairs, the first sunlight touching the east windows. When he crossed the kitchen to the back porch, he glimpsed Maggie in the pantry. He pumped a pan of cold water and washed, and before he finished drying, Maggie came out of the house.

"I'll have breakfast for you right away," Maggie said.

"I'll eat in the cook shack," he said.

"This is where you belong," she said stubbornly. "Your father never ate with the crew."

He grinned at her, then his face turned grave. "I'm not in quite the same shape Dad was." He jerked his thumb in the general direction of Ann's upstairs room. "What's between her and Colter?"

"Nothing on her side," Maggie answered without hesitation, "but a lot on his. I've seen him look at her, even before Sherm died. It wasn't decent, Jim. Just wasn't decent."

"Keep your eyes open today," he said. "Colter might be back."

"I wish you'd killed him," she said bitterly. "I wish you had."

"So do I," he said.

He walked to the bunkhouse, glancing around with sudden nervousness, and condemned himself at once. He didn't expect Colter to be hiding around a corner of the barn or the bunkhouse or the new shed, yet he was afraid. This was the way it would be as long as Colter was alive. Every day. Every hour.

Jim took Castleman lightly. He could afford to as long as he wasn't in town, for he felt reasonably certain that Castleman would not come here after him. Colter would. He could have gone for his gun yesterday. The fact that he hadn't demonstrated the kind of man he was.

Alec Torrin was done eating when Jim sat down at the long table in the cook shack. He said, "Saddle Sundown for me," and Alec nodded and left. Sugar started Jim's flapjacks and brought the coffeepot to where Jim sat and filled his cup. The cook's mustache drooped more than ever, his long bony face seemed more melancholy than ever, and the worried uncertainty in Jim continued to grow.

He wondered if his father had ever faced anything like this. He remembered Sherman Dunn as a big, handsome man who always carried himself with great dignity, and only a few like Judge Riddle and Luke Dilly ever presumed to break down the barrier that his poise seemed to automatically build around him. But the earliest memories he had of his father were that of a man well into his forties. What was he like when he was twenty-three and filled with the uncertainties of youth? That, Jim knew, was a question he would never be able to answer.

By the time he finished breakfast, Alec was waiting in front with Sundown. Jim asked, "How does he feel this morning?"

"Frisky," Alec said. "Watch him when the seat of your pants hits the saddle."

"I will," Jim said. "You head for town and get that wire off to Luke, then get back here and stay here. Keep your Winchester handy. If there is a ruckus, get to the house and look out for the women. I'll probably stay up there with Lennie tonight. I figure Colter will wait long enough for us to get boogery, but don't take any chances."

"I won't," Alec said.

Jim patted Sundown's sleek neck, wanting to ask a question, but afraid he would show his feelings by asking it. Then he decided it didn't make any difference what Alec thought, so he asked, "Was Dad ever afraid of anything? That you knew of, I mean?"

Alec's sunburned face took on a strange expression. He glanced at Jim, then looked away and dug a toe of his boot through the dust of the yard. "Funny you'd ask that. I was just thinking about it. The only time I ever knew Sherm to be scared was just before he got killed. He didn't say anything, mind you, but it was working on him. I dunno what it was, but I had a hunch he wanted to fire Colter and was afraid to tackle it. Maybe Colter saw it coming. Might be why Sherm died when he did."

Just a guess, Jim thought. Something could have happened between him and Ann that made him afraid she'd leave him. Maybe he'd told her he was going to fire Colter and they'd quarreled over it. But here was another question that would probably not be answered. He would never know, either, if Ann had made his father as happy as she pretended.

"Well, better go," he said, and swung into the saddle.

One minute Sundown had been standing there, perfectly docile, the next he was unwinding in a great cloud of dust, and Alec was howling, "Ride 'em, cowboy." Then Sundown headed south on the dead run, not slowing down until he hit the mesa hill. He snorted as if he was happy to be alive and have Jim in the saddle.

Jim rode due south, dropping into arroyos and climbing out again, crossing cedar-covered flats that tilted up slightly toward the divide in front of him. Then he began to climb steadily, the trail twisting through a heavy growth of service berry brush, and now and then he had to pull up and let Sundown blow.

This was Box D's winter range, with fair grass and narrow canyons on both sides of him that offered protection during winter storms. He rode on through scrub oak, remembering how he had fought his way through this jungle every year at roundup time, and at night his body had been as sore and battered as it was now from Bud Colter's fist.

Other memories crowded in, of branding fires and the bellow of fretful cows and the bawl of hurt calves as the hot iron sizzled through thick hair and burned the Box D into their hides, of Sugar's meals around the chuck wagon and the tall tales spun by Luke Dilly and Lennie Nolan and the rest, and above everything else, that spirit of belonging which could never be measured by the tangible standards.

He went on, still climbing, and presently he was in the quaking asps, their tiny leaves turned orange. Some of them had dropped and dried, and now rustled under Sundown's hoofs. The wind rushed through the trees, biting at Jim and sending the leaves into a twirling dance, or breaking them free so they drifted through the air like thin, light five-dollar gold pieces.

He reached a park and reining up, looked back. He could barely make out the Box D buildings, the walls on both sides of the valley reduced by distance to a height of a few inches, and on past Ruby Mesa he could see Cairo, cut down to the size of a little girl's play town, and still beyond the Uncompahgre were the 'dobe hills, a faint streak of gray at the far side of the valley. Directly below him was the maze of canyons and arroyos above which he had threaded his way by holding to the ridges.

A big country, he thought as he rode on. Above him a hawk swooped down and away, then he was in a belt of close-growing spruce that laid a chill twilight against the trail. Somewhere off to his right a noisy jay squalled a bitter diatribe against life.

Again he fell into a somber mood as he thought how a man could see only the superficial, the dark green of the spruce and the bright orange of the aspen and the splash of blue that was the jay as he streaked from one tree to another. But beneath all of this was the eternal war, of life against life, with the innocent snowshoe rabbit having only one defense against the carnivores: his color. The coyotes were Frank Castlemans, the wolves Bud Colters. But what was Ann Dunn?

He shook his head, not liking this kind of thinking, and was glad when he came out of the spruce into the park that held the line cabin. This was very close to the divide. He looked up at the tall sandstone cliff just above the cabin with the collection of boulders along the top that had always reminded him of a row of eggs laid there by some prehistoric monster, half bird, half animal.

He laughed, the tension giving way now that he was in the sunshine. Lennie's spare horses were staked out near the base of the sandstone cliff. He saw no other sign of life. He called, "Lennie," but there was no answer. He dismounted in front of the cabin, untied the sack of grub he had brought, and carried it inside. The interior of the cabin was neat and clean. He remembered that was characteristic of Lennie, a bachelor under forty thoroughly set in his ways. Neatness and order had always been a fetish with him.

Jim loosened the cinch and let Sundown drink at a pool just below the spring in front of the cabin, then he led the bay down to the lower end of the park where the grass was good and staked him out. He pulled the saddle off and tossed it down, deciding there was no sense in riding out to find Lennie. He might be anywhere along the divide.

Lennie's job was to haze any Box D cows back that showed an inclination to cross over to the other side which was XM summer range, an outfit with headquarters on the San Miguel. There never had been any trouble between them, largely because Sherman Dunn had seen to it there was never any cause for trouble.

Jim built a fire and cooked his dinner, then sat in the doorway and smoked a cigarette, wondering how Lennie could stay by himself all summer. But, as Alec had said, probably it was easier than staying on the Box D and having Colter needle him for one thing or another. Jim finished his cigarette and stretched out in the sun, his Stetson over his eyes, and dropped off to sleep. He woke when he heard a horse coming in, and Lennie's voice, "On your feet, bucko. Let's see what you look like."

He got up, ashamed. If Colter or one of his men had caught him like this, he'd be dead before he woke up. He said, "Howdy, Lennie."

"I'll be damned." Lennie leaned forward in the saddle and blinked. "Yes sir, I'll be damned." He rode up, his hand extended. "How are you, Jim?"

"All in one piece so far," Jim said as he shook hands, "but we've got trouble."

"Been coming ever since Sherm cashed in," Lennie said. "Before that, as far as that goes. Back to the day Sherm hired Bud Colter. Well, heat up the coffee. I'll be in soon as I unsaddle."

He came into the cabin a moment later, a stocky man with a moonlike face that scorched a bright red every summer but never tanned. He was about as unlike a cowboy in appearance as a man could be, but his appearance was deceiving. He was a good hand, and Jim had always supposed that when Luke Dilly got too old to run the outfit, Lennie would be in line. He would have been, Jim thought, if Ann Dunn hadn't moved in.

"Well it's good to see you, Jim," Lennie said. "Sure didn't expect you, but I should have."

"Judge Riddle got hold of me," Jim said, and told Lennie what had happened while the coffee heated.

When he finished, Lennie rose and poured the coffee. "A man can't live this way, Jim. No use trying. You'll see Colter behind every bush; you'll hear a gun being cocked behind every rock. It'll put bees in your bonnet as sure as you're a foot high."

"I know it," Jim said, "but what can I do? I haven't got a thing to go to Hank Watrous about, and it wouldn't do any good if I did."

"Watrous?" Lennie laughed. "Might as well put a star on one of the scarecrows in Maggie's garden." He stared at the coffee in front of him and automatically reached for tobacco and paper. "Colter's a bastard, Jim. I never knew another man you could call a bastard and be one hundred per cent right like you can with Colter. He had his eyes on the Box D from the minute he got here. Why Sherm couldn't see it I just don't know. Had his eyes on Miz Dunn, too."

Lennie struck a match, and lighted a cigarette. "Colter won't pull out. Not till you're dead and Miz Dunn builds a fire under his tail. Severe won't neither. Rest of 'em might. Only one thing you can do and I'll help you. We'll hunt 'em down, Jim, hunt 'em down like you would sheep-killing dogs. I don't know 'bout Castleman. Maybe he can be bluffed, but not Colter and Severe. You've just got to kill 'em."

"I've sent for Luke Dilly," Jim said. "Winter's coming on and we've got a ranch to run. We can't hunt Colter and work a ranch at the same time."

Lennie drank his coffee and put the cup down. "All right, let Luke run the ranch. Him and Alec can take care of most things. Cows are drifting down now. A storm's coming, the way they act. They'll be down in the scrub oak by the time it hits, so don't worry about 'em. We'll hire some gun slingers. We'll go up into the mining camps. I know two, three real good boys we can get."

He got up and grinned at Jim. "I'm telling you, boy, there ain't a thing on this green earth I'd rather do than get Bud Colter in my sights and a good reason to pull the trigger, which I reckon I've got. Now I ain't telling you how to run this shebang, but the way I see it, there's no need of me staying up here. I say close the cabin, take the horses down, and I'll start looking for some gun slingers." He flipped his cigarette into the yard. "What do you say?"

"Jake with me if you can find the men . . ."

Lennie was already through the door headed for his horse. A rifle cracked from the sandstone cliff above the cabin and Lennie spun and fell. The rifle sounded again. Jim reached the door in two strides; he saw Lennie's shirt give with the impact of the second bullet, and he knew Lennie was dead. He took one instinctive step past the door when he realized this was exactly what they wanted and he jumped back as another bullet breathed past in front of him.

He slammed the door and barred it. The top of the sandstone cliff seemed to erupt into flame as bullets slapped into the earth roof and rattled the tin chimney and buried themselves with dull *thwacks* into the logs.

Lennie's rifle was in the corner. Jim picked it up, and whirling, searched for a loophole through which to shoot, but there wasn't any. He could knock out the chinking and slip the rifle barrel between the logs, but it was impossible to tilt it up enough to fire accurately at the men atop the sandstone cliff.

He stood in the middle of the room, not knowing what to do. He was trapped. If he went outside he was a dead man. There was one window on the downhill side of the cabin. He looked out but saw nothing except the dark wall of spruce that surrounded the clearing. He wouldn't have the slightest chance of crossing the fifty yards of clearing to the timber. He'd be cut down before he'd gone ten feet.

This was like Colter, he thought, to hide up there and kill Lennie and wait for him. It would be easy enough to dispose of his and Lennie's bodies, then go back to the Box D and take over with Ann's blessing. Jim swore and shook his fist at the top of the cliff; he thought of Lennie, lying out there, killed without any chance to fight for his life, and he swore again until he was out of breath.

He sat down and put his Winchester on the floor,

feeling absolutely helpless. There was nothing he could do, not a single thing unless they rushed the cabin, and they weren't the kind of men who would do that. The firing had stopped. They might try to burn him out, but the earth roof wouldn't burn and it would be difficult to start a fire against the logs. Slowly sanity began replacing the panic. All he had to do was wait until dark and make a run for it. That wouldn't be long, maybe an hour.

Something hit the ground outside, something so heavy that it shook the cabin. He ran to the window, but could see nothing except a faint stain of dust in the air. He wheeled to the door and opened it. His breath went out of his lungs as if he had been struck in the stomach with a club. He leaned against the door casing, too weak to move.

One of the egglike boulders from the top of the cliff had been rolled off the rim. It had not missed the cabin by more than ten feet. The next one might not miss. His choice was clear. He could make a run for it and get shot, or stay here and be smashed to blood and pulp in the wreckage of a splintered cabin.

Chapter XIII

Colter got out of bed with an effort on the morning after his fight with Jim Dunn. He could not remember when he had hurt in so many places. His face, covered by purple bruises and ugly scabs, stung when he washed. He glanced briefly at the mirror and turned away at once, ashamed of his appearance and strongly tempted to go back to bed and stay there. But he had a great deal to do and not much time, so he swallowed his pride and went downstairs.

He had breakfast in the hotel dining room with Crip Lannigen. As the waitress turned away after taking their order, Lannigen said, "Wonder what shape Castleman's in . . ."

"Shut up, you fool," Colter said in a low tone. After the girl disappeared through the swinging door into the kitchen, he asked, "You want our business spread all over town?"

"I just didn't think," Lannigen said.

"You'd better start thinking," Colter said, "or we'll all be dancing on air."

After that Lannigen said nothing until they got their horses from the stable, Shep Hofferd looking at Colter's face curiously, but restraining his impulse to ask what had happened. After

Lannigen and Colter mounted and were in the street, Lannigen asked, "Where we headed?"

"Box D," Colter answered. "We'll get Watrous to go along."

He gave no explanation, and Lannigen, inhibited by habit, did not question him, although his puzzled expression plainly showed he did not understand. They reined up in front of the courthouse. Colter said, "Go see if Watrous is in his office." Lannigen stepped down, but he did not go ten steps until Colter called, "Come on back, Crip. He's coming now."

They waited in front of the courthouse, Colter watching Watrous who yawned and rubbed his face, and apparently seeing the two men for the first time, called, "Howdy, gents. What fetches you to town this time of day?"

"Dunn fired us and ran us off the ranch yesterday," Colter said. "We want you to ride out there with us so we can get our stuff. If we go alone, Dunn will blow us out of our saddles before we get within fifty yards of the place." He paused, letting this sink in, then added, "That Jim Dunn is a bad actor, Hank. An outlaw, if I ever saw one."

Watrous pulled at an ear, undecided. "Bill Royal was telling me the same thing. Said he knocked hell out of Frank Castleman yesterday for no reason at all. But I dunno 'bout riding out there, Bud. I've got a wife and three kids . . ."

"You should have thought of that when you ran

for sheriff," Colter said. "You'll go, or I'll see Judge Riddle and tell him . . ."

Watrous had been staring up at Colter's face, made ugly by temper as well as the bruises and scabs. Now he broke in, "All right, Bud, I'll go. Wait'll I get my horse."

He joined them a few minutes later, riding his ancient gray mare. They crossed the bridge and took the Ruby Mesa road, Colter wondering what Watrous would do if he ever needed a fast horse. He had not taken a posse out of town since he'd been elected. If anything happened that forced him to organize one, it would probably be hours before he could get a bunch of men who were well enough mounted to take out of town.

"Sure worried 'bout my youngest," Watrous said, and yawned again. "Dunno what I'm gonna do for sleep. Cried almost all night, he did."

Neither Colter nor Lannigen showed any interest, and Watrous was silent the rest of the way to the Box D. He fell behind, taking Colter's and Lannigen's dust, riding like a sack of wool in the saddle. He was inadequate and futile, Colter told himself, and he didn't have an ounce of sand in his craw. As far as protection went, he was worse than nothing.

But even Hank Watrous was not entirely predictable. As the three of them approached the ranch, Colter saw Sugar Sanders leave the cook shack with a Winchester in his hands and run into

144

the house. A moment later the front door slammed open and Maggie O'Boyle and Sugar stepped out, Maggie holding a double-barreled shotgun and Sugar his rifle.

"Stay where you are, Colter," Maggie yelled. "You come any closer and I'll blow your purty head right off your shoulders."

"Why, she's downright unreasonable," Watrous said. "Stay here, Bud. I'll talk to her."

Colter and Lannigen reined up and Watrous put his gray into a jolting trot. Lannigen snickered. "I'll bet that mare is purty good hitched to a plow."

Watrous stopped in front of the house, talked briefly to Maggie, and then waved for Colter and Lannigen to come on. When Colter reached the house and dismounted, Maggie glowered at him as if still strongly tempted to carry out her threat. She said, "I sure wish Jim was here. He'd finish what he started yesterday if he was."

"And go to jail," Watrous said. "Where is he?"

"Went up to the line cabin to see Lennie," Sugar said. "Won't be back until tomorrow."

"Pack up your junk and git," Maggie said.

"Go ahead, Crip." Colter nodded at Lannigen. "I want to see Mrs. Dunn."

"Oh no you don't," Maggie bellowed.

Ann raised a window in her private parlor and looked out. "What do you want, Colter?"

He tipped his head back and looked up. He had

never seen her more tantalizingly beautiful than she was at that moment, and he was immediately conscious of his battered face and the fact that he had not shaved this morning. He said, "I've got some things to discuss with you. Our wages for October, for one thing."

"Go see Judge Riddle," she said.

She didn't want to see him, he thought. He burst out, "There's something else, ma'am. I don't think you want it talked about in front of anybody else."

She hesitated, plainly not liking it, and Maggie said, "You purty piece of scum, why don't you get out of here?"

"Let him come up, Maggie," Ann said. "I'm sure it won't take long."

Colter walked across the porch and through the front room and up the stairs, the resentment and bitterness that had been in him since the fight with Dunn now flaming into red fury and crowding out his sense of logic. The door of her parlor was open, and he stomped in, his spurs jingling.

"Shut the window," he ordered.

She obeyed and turned to face him, holding him away from her with a cold smile. "Sherm's boy surprised you, didn't he? You expected a drunken, sponging, crawling weakling, but he's a long ways from that, isn't he?" He stood looking at her, saying nothing, and she added, "Your face shows you found out, all right. You never took a whipping like that before, did you, Bud?"

He made one step toward her, then stopped. She was not wearing the black silk dress he liked so much, but a pink one with a row of tiny bows down the front between her breasts, quite tight at her waist and hips, a dress which he had not seen before and one that was plainly designed to attract a man.

He licked his lips. "Come here. I haven't kissed you for a long time."

"Not since Sherm and I were married." She shook her head. "No, Colter. We're done. And you're done as far as Box D is concerned."

He had known that from the instant he had entered the room. She had put on that dress for Jim Dunn, probably not knowing he would be gone all night. She was still smiling, coldly, with no hint of the warm promise he had seen so many times on her lips and in her eyes.

He hated her then almost as much as he hated Jim Dunn. He gripped the butt of his gun, thinking he would rather kill her than let Dunn have her. Then his hand fell away. Later, maybe, but not now. He had never seen her more beautiful and more unattainable, and so desire and frustration were all mixed up in him until his habitual calculating self-control was swept aside.

"You're going to marry me and you'll kiss me again, all right," he said, and started toward her. "What do you think I've been waiting around for?"

She plainly had expected this. Now a short-barreled, nickel-plated gun was in her hand. "This isn't much of a gun, Bud, and I'm not much of a shot, but at this distance I couldn't help killing you." He stopped, and she said, "I don't suppose it ever occurred to a man in love with himself as much as you are that I wouldn't marry him."

He stared at her, realizing how perfectly she had seen through him. There were many times when he did not understand her, but she had one trait he understood perfectly. She'd had a hard life before she had come to the Box D, so hard that she never wanted to go back. She would look out for herself no matter what it cost her, or him.

"You think you'll get him, don't you?" he asked.

"I think so," she said.

"Even at your age?"

"I wasn't too young for his father, and I'm not too old for him. I paid off my obligation to you, Bud. I owe you nothing. Now get out of the country and leave me alone."

He looked at the deadly little gun in her hand. He thought of all the women he'd had, of other women he could have had, Bud Colter who had not grown any older with the years, Bud Colter who had only to crook his finger and bring a woman running. But not Ann Delaney. Ann Dunn now. So, because he could not have her, he wanted her above all others.

"You'll never get him," Colter burst out. "By

God, I'll see he finds out what you were . . ."

"I've already told him," she said. "I knew what you'd do. Now I've had enough, Bud. Get out."

He wheeled and strode to the door, then he stopped and stared at her, filling his eyes with what might be the last look he'd ever have of her. He said, "I'm telling you again you'll never get him. I won't leave this country till he's a dead man." He left then, down the stairs and through the front door, ignoring Maggie who was still standing there with her shotgun in her hands, and went on out to the bunkhouse.

Lannigen had filled his war sack and tied it behind his saddle. Sugar apparently had returned to the cook shack. Alec Torrin was nowhere in sight. Watrous followed Colter into the bunkhouse and watched him gather up his shaving gear and a few other odds and ends.

"What are you boys gonna do now?" Watrous asked.

"I don't know." Colter strode past the sheriff, tied his sack behind the saddle, and mounted. "Crip and me ain't going back to town with you, Hank. Thanks for coming out."

"Glad to," Watrous said, and swung aboard his mare.

"I just hope I can keep Dunn from shooting me in the back," Colter said. "He'll go gunning for Castleman and then me, if I know that bastard."

He rode down valley, Lannigen beside him.

149

Lannigen said, "I wish I knew what was in that head of your'n, Bud."

"Plenty," Colter said. "We'll be rich. You'll see. Right now we're going after Dunn. He's up there with Lennie. We'll get that ornery son, too. He always was a little too smart for his britches."

Half an hour later they left the valley, riding toward the divide. Presently Monument Rock came into sight, a tall spire of red sandstone, and by forcing their horses as hard as they could, reached the cabin at the foot of the rock by noon.

Toy Severe hunkered in the shade, saying nothing until they dismounted, although Colter was sure he had been watching them for the past half hour. He was like a small, vicious bird, Colter thought, waiting to peck the eyes out of his enemy when the sign was right.

Sometimes there was a question in Colter's mind as to the identity of Severe's enemies. A second question bothered him even more. How long could he hold his position of leadership? Severe would take over the instant he thought he could. You could never be sure of men like Lannigen and the Masons, not sure at all if Severe came up with some rich promises.

"A mite slow, ain't you, Bud?" Severe asked.

"No," Colter said.

He was edgy and he knew it. He had been going over in his thoughts the things Ann had said to him. Now his mind was nothing but a receptacle for the ashes of his burned-out plans. If he had made them work, she would have come to him gladly, but they hadn't worked, so there was nothing left but to put a bullet into Jim Dunn.

Severe got up, ground out his cigarette with the toe of his boot, then motioned toward the interior of the cabin. "Grub's ready. We figured you and Crip would be along."

Lannigen had already led the horses toward the creek that ran past the cabin. Colter went inside. Ash Mason was sprawled on a bunk asleep. Del was standing by the stove frying flapjacks. Frank Castleman sat in a chair, his hands and feet tied.

"Sit down'n eat," Del said cheerfully. "Ash got his belly full, but Frank over yonder don't care for my cooking, seems like."

Castleman broke into a torrent of vitriolic curses. Colter said, "Shut up now. I had the boys bring you out here so you'd have a chance to take care of Dunn. That's what you wanted, wasn't it?

"Not now it ain't," Castleman yelled. "If you think I'm gonna forget what them Mason idiots done to me, you're loco. You're the one I'm gonna get if I ever get out of these ropes."

Colter wheeled to the bunk where Ash Mason lay and prodded him awake, then turned back to the table and sat down. He said, "Saddle your horse and Del's. We're going after Dunn soon as me and Crip eat."

Ash shook the cobwebs of sleep out of his head,

grunting something, and went outside. Lannigen came in and sat down at the table, saying, "It'll push us to get to that line cabin before dark."

"We'll push," Colter said. "Get your eating done."

By the time they finished, Ash Mason had the horses in front of the cabin. Colter went outside. He said, "Watch Castleman, Toy."

"Sure, Boss," Severe said in a faintly mocking tone.

Colter led the way up the slope from the cabin through the aspens. He'd have it out with Severe before long. They had to get it into the open one way or the other. Severe had something in his mind. All right, Colter would listen to what it was, and then he'd see. But one thing was gratifying. Lannigen and the Masons had followed him without any argument.

They stopped to rest their horses often, too often to suit Colter, but his and Lannigen's mounts had already been ridden hard. They reached the divide in late afternoon, Colter pulling up to get his bearings, then struck out along the top toward the sandstone cliff that rose above the line cabin. Dunn and Lennie would want to talk, so they'd be in the cabin. Or outside. This should go off without a hitch.

Half an hour later they pulled up behind the cliff and leaving the reins dragging, clambered to the top. Not much of a climb from this side, but an impossible one from the other. Colter said, "No shooting till I say so."

"Won't be good shooting light much longer," Ash said. Del put a hand against a boulder and rocked it. "Be fun to roll a few of these over. If Dunn's inside, that'd fetch him out."

Colter was looking over the rim now. No one was in sight, but smoke was rising from the chimney. He saw Sundown at the lower end of the clearing. Lennie's horses were all in sight, so both men must be inside.

He turned his head. "Sooner or later they'll have to come out," he said. "We'll get both of them . . ."

Ash Mason cut loose twice with his rifle. Colter looked down in time to see Lennie fall, then Dunn appeared and jumped back just as Del fired and missed. Colter fisted his hands and cursed. If they had just waited . . . But all three of them were firing now, like kids with a bunch of firecrackers on the Fourth of July.

"Stop it," Colter shouted. "Trying to use up every shell you've got?"

They looked at him a little shamefaced. Del said, "Maybe we jumped the gun."

"Jumped it," Colter said bitterly. "You sure did."

Lannigen was teetering one of the boulders. "Bud, come here. We can get this one over. A couple more wouldn't take much heaving on 'em. We'll make splinters out of that cabin, or scare Dunn into making a run for it."

Colter put a hand on the boulder and rocked it, then looked speculatively at the cabin. "All right," he said. "See if you can get it started. I'll watch."

He moved along the rim, his eyes on the cabin door. He doubted that the boulder would hit the cabin, but Dunn below wouldn't know what the next one would do. Colter could imagine how he'd feel if he were down there. He wouldn't stay. He'd run, and he was reasonably sure that's what Dunn would do. He listened to the grunting and swearing, and then the big rock gave and went hurtling down the nearly sheer slope.

"Hell, it missed," Lannigen said in disgust. "All that work for nothing."

"I don't think so," Colter said. "One more will bring him out of there like a rabbit going for his hole."

He laughed softly, thinking of the sheer, abject terror that must be in Jim Dunn, and then he ran his fingers across his bruised face, and laughed again.

CHAPTER XIV

The minutes that Jim Dunn spent in the line cabin after Lennie Nolan's death were the longest minutes he had ever spent in his life. By standing in the doorway, he could look up at the rim without being seen and thus did not draw the ambushers' fire. If he took an additional step, he would come into view and they'd cut him down. So he remained there, looking up and listened to the sound of rock scraping on rock as another boulder was laboriously nudged closer to the rim.

Now and then a rifle cracked, the bullet making a dull *plock* as it buried itself in a log. The idea was to keep him nailed down until the second boulder was dislodged. He had no idea how long it would take, but he did know that within another half hour or so the dusk light would be so thin that accurate shooting from the rim would be impossible. He'd make a run for it then, he decided, although he was perfectly aware that one of them might have ridden down around the cliff and was watching from the protection of the spruce that surrounded the clearing.

Jim had faced death many times. In Las Vegas when he had stood in the street and knocked a bank robber out of his saddle, the bullets flying all around him. In El Paso when he had shot a gambler across a card table before the man could fire his derringer. In Cairo the night Frank Castleman had tried to kill him. There were other times, too, when life or death depended on what happened within a few seconds.

But this was different. He was faced with the choice of running and dying, or staying and dying, and what hurt the most was the fact that he couldn't fight back. It was like shooting a grouse out of a tree, and he was the grouse. All they had to do was to keep at it until they got him.

He wondered if Castleman was up there with them. Colter, certainly, Colter who had undoubtedly killed his father, a murder that would go unavenged. He thought of Ginny and the loneliness that had been his through the three years he was gone and the dreams he had dreamed about her. The Box D, too. It would be his now if . . .

All thought processes stopped. He was aware of nothing but the big rock that toppled over the rim and strength went out of his belly and knees and he began to sag. Time ribboned out until this second was squeezed into an eternity. The boulder grew in size until it blotted out the rim and the sky. Suddenly he began to breathe again. The rock was going to fall short just as the first one had.

Then he froze. The boulder struck a ledge with a tremendous crash that started a small avalanche pouring down the side of the cliff; it bounced up, reached a crest and seemed to hang there in space, then started down.

Jim hung to the door casing with both hands, eyes on the boulder, and for this one horrible moment he thought it was going to strike squarely in the middle of the cabin's roof. Instead it went completely over the cabin, missing it by not more than two feet, and hit the ground with a terrific thud that jarred the pots and pans in the cabin and raised a cloud of dust.

Relief was a strange, aching weakness in him. One had fallen short, one had gone too far. Would the third strike in between? He could not expect luck to go on running his way. He heard a derisive laugh, and a man called down, "We've got some more up here." Then a shot came from the other end of the clearing, and another, and Alec Torrin yelled, "Come a-running, Jim. We'll keep 'em down on that rim so they can't shoot."

Sweat had broken out all over Jim's body. It ran in a dribbling stream down his face and back and dampened the hairs on his chest and belly. He crouched there in the doorway, too weak to move. He heard Alec again, "Come on, Jim, if you're there. I tell you we can make 'em keep their heads down."

He came out of it then, ran out and picked up Lennie's body, and carried it the length of the clearing. It slowed him up, and when he reached the timber, he was so tired he was stumbling, but he could not have left the body there. One of the boulders might have fallen on Lennie and crushed him so completely they could never find enough to bury. It did not occur to him until he laid the body down that they would roll no more boulders now that he was out of the cabin.

He leaned against a tree trunk, panting. Alec and Sugar were both there. Sugar had saddled

Sundown and was holding the reins. Jim wiped sweat from his face. He said, "The bastards shot Lennie without any warning. He just stepped out of the cabin. I was right behind him. If they'd waited a minute they'd have got me, too."

Alec swore. "Colter came out to the Box D this morning with Lannigen and Watrous. I was in town, and when I got back, I heard about it. This damned fool Sugar told 'em you was up here, so I knew Colter would be after you."

Sugar was staring at Lennie's body, tears rolling down his gaunt cheeks into his drooping mustache. "I killed him, Jim," he said. "If I hadn't told 'em . . ."

"No sense blaming yourself." Jim laid a hand on his shoulder. "We're all to blame more or less. I should have shot Colter yesterday like I would have shot a skunk that walked into the bunkhouse. Looks like I shouldn't have come up here either." He swallowed, wanting to say Ann Dunn was to blame, or his father for letting her talk him into firing Luke Dilly and hiring Colter. But there was no use going back over water that had flowed over the dam so long ago.

He heard horses' hoofs on rock. They were coming down around the edge of the cliff. He was out of the trap. Whatever happened now, he didn't want Alec and Sugar to wind up the same way Lennie Nolan had.

"Get your horses and Lennie off the trail," he

said. "Stay in the spruce, far enough so they won't see you when they go by. Colter's after me, and I aim to give him a run."

"You ain't gonna do no such thing," Alec snapped.

"Do what I tell you," Jim said, and mounting Sundown, started toward the Box D.

He could still hear the horses coming down the steep slant at the edge of the cliff. He threw back a taunting yell so they would know where he was, then put Sundown into a run. Presently he pulled up, for it was twilight now. He was in the scrub oak, the trail dropping fast. He waited until he could hear them coming again, then threw out another long, derisive yell, and went on.

By the time it was completely dark he was in the cedars. There was no moon, but the sky was filled with stars, and now that he was in the open, the country seemed magnified both in depth and distance. Canyons dropping off on both sides of the trail were bottomless, and on ahead of him across a series of ridges and arroyos he could see the pinpoint of light that was the Box D.

He had no idea how many men were behind him, or how close they were, and he could not keep from worrying about Alec and Sugar. If they had waited long enough, they would be in no danger. On the other hand, they might have hurried to give him help if he needed it. In that case, there was a good chance they were in trouble. So he waited, listening intently. He had not heard any shooting, but he had not heard his pursuers for several minutes, either.

He waited for what seemed a long time, although it could not have been more than ten or fifteen minutes, then he heard them coming down the trail, slowly as if afraid they might ride into an ambush. He rode on, shaking his head as he considered that point. If he were another man, a Castleman or a Colter, he would pull off the trail and wait beside a bushy cedar and shoot them as they rode by. But he couldn't do it, and there was no use to even think about it. A man was what he was; he fought by his standards, not by another's.

The men behind were riding faster now and beginning to close the gap. Jim put his horse down the steep, short drops into the arroyos and out again, Sundown grunting and straining as he made the climbs, then followed the snakelike trail that twisted along the ridge tops and dropped again.

The trail was rocky, the gelding's shoes striking sparks repeatedly. Jim made no effort to throw the men off the track. He reined up once to briefly rest Sundown, and from the sound of pursuit, he was convinced there were not more than two or three of them.

He tipped down off the mesa hill, once again throwing back that derisive yell, knowing it would infuriate Colter. He put Sundown into a gallop across the flat, glad that the lights in the house were out. He pulled up in the yard, swung down, stripped saddle from his horse and gave him a slap on the rump, then ran toward the cotton-woods in front of the house.

Upstairs a lamp came to life. He yelled, "Douse it. Douse it." The lamp died instantly. The front screen banged shut and Maggie called, "Where are you, Jim? I've got a rifle. If they're coming . . ."

"Sure they're coming," he shouted at her. "Get back inside."

Again the screen door slammed, but he wasn't sure she had obeyed. He could barely make them out, just two, coming in across the flat, and he realized he was breathing hard. One of them must be Colter. He had a chance to end it now. He crouched there at the base of the cottonwood's trunk, his gun in his hand, then they veered off, riding in an arc in front of the house and coming no closer.

They began firing, apparently just at the house. He fired back, a gesture of defiance as much as anything else. They were too far out. Even if they had been closer, the starlight was so thin that a hit would have been nothing more than an accident.

He reloaded just as Maggie cut loose from the front porch with the Winchester. He grinned. That was like her. If there was a fight, Maggie O'Boyle was buying her share. Now the riders were heading down valley, and Jim dropped his gun into the holster, calling, "They've gone, Maggie." She stopped shooting, and presently the sound of hoofbeats faded and finally died.

Silence, except for the wind that rattled the limbs of the cottonwoods over Jim's head. Cold, now that he was motionless. He hadn't thought about it as he'd come down off the divide, and he remembered Lennie saying there would be a storm, that the cows smelled it coming.

From the porch Maggie called, "You all right, Jim?"

"Sure." He went to her. "Who were you shooting at?"

"Just shooting," she said. "I figured Colter was out there, and I didn't want that spalpeen to think this was a one-man show."

"You're worth two men," Jim said, and patted her on the back.

The screen opened and shut, and he heard Ann ask, "What happened, Jim?"

"They killed Lennie Nolan," he answered, "and they'd have got me if Alec and Sugar hadn't showed up."

He heard her gasp, then she came to him and put her arms around him. "But you're all right, Jim?" She felt of his face and ran her hands on down his chest. "Jim, Jim, when will this be over?"

"When Colter's dead," he said. "No sooner."

"Luke Dilly's coming Sunday," Maggie said. "He's bringing three men with him. He wired you. A kid fetched it out from town."

"I wish he was coming tomorrow," Jim said.

162

Ann was still there, an arm around him. He wanted to shove her away from him, or thought he did, then he wasn't sure. He felt her shiver, whether from cold or fear he did not know. She said, "I liked Lennie, Jim. So did Sherm. I'm sorry it happened."

"I'm sorry about a lot of things that have happened," he said. "Some of them I just don't savvy."

"Colter was here this morning," she said. "He insisted on seeing me. I told him to go away and stay away, that I'd kept my part of the bargain and I owed him nothing." She shivered again. "I'm scared, Jim. He said he wouldn't leave the country until you were dead."

He said nothing for a moment, but he was thinking that Colter's idea was clear enough. He had not given her up. He would never give her up as long as he was alive. Once Jim Dunn was out of the way, she would want him back. That must be, Jim told himself, the way Colter's thinking went.

"Go to bed," Jim said. "You're cold."

He stepped off the porch and walked across the yard to the bunkhouse. He could not risk going to sleep. For a time he walked around just to keep awake. He went into the cook shack and built a fire and made coffee, fumbling around in the dark because he was afraid to light a lamp.

He drank the scalding coffee; it hit his stomach with a shock and jolted him awake, and all the time he was thinking about Ginny and wondering how he could bring her to live here with Ann still in the house. Was there a way to get rid of Ann? He was more concerned about Maggie than Ann. He didn't want to offend her. He owed her too much.

He went outside and sat down on the steps, staring across the valley at the black line of the mesa hill and hearing the coyotes' call from some ridge top off to the west where he had been a few hours before. But they made no real impression upon him; they were vaguely seen and vaguely heard, for he was thinking of his early boyhood when his mother was alive. Not young and handsome as Ann was, just a good, hard-working woman who had loved him and looked out for him, and tried to get along with Sherman Dunn.

It had never been the same after his mother had died. Just Maggie who did the best she could and made life bearable for him. Thus he completed his circle of thinking, and he told himself again that he could not offend Maggie, even if it meant putting Ginny off. The trouble was Ginny wouldn't understand. He'd see the Judge tomorrow. There were several things he wanted to know. Why the Judge needed him was one.

He heard them coming and rose and walked away from the cook shack, listening. Presently he called, "Alec? Sugar?"

"Sure is," Alec sang out. "We was wondering if you made it."

They rode in, Alec leading one of Lennie's horses, Lennie's body tied across the saddle. Jim said, "Guess I'll go to bed. We'll bury Lennie tomorrow afternoon. You dig the grave in the morning. I'll fetch a coffin from town."

Alec and Sugar stood in front of him, sore and stiff from the long ride. It was near dawn, and for a moment the three of them were silent and motionless, here in this ebb tide hour when the pulse of life slows until death is close. It was with them now. Jim knew they were all thinking of Lennie.

"Me or Alec will stay up," Sugar said. "I can't sleep no how."

"We go coyote hunting after the funeral," Alec said. "That it?"

"That's it," Jim said. "On Box D range, the way I figure it."

He walked toward the house, and when he went into the front room, he heard Maggie's fretful breathing. He found her on the leather couch, asleep, her Winchester on the floor. He shook her awake. "Go on to bed, Maggie," he said. "We won't have any more trouble tonight."

He climbed the stairs to his room, and he thought again of Maggie who believed in Ann. Just the three of them now, Maggie and Alec and Sugar. He would talk to Maggie tomorrow. Maybe she would understand about Ginny and him, and tell him what to do.

CHAPTER XV

Jim left early the following morning for Cairo in the spring wagon. His first stop was at the preacher's house on the way into town to ask if he would conduct the funeral service that afternoon for Lennie Nolan.

"Of course," the preacher said. "At what hour?"

"Three."

The preacher's name was Jason Monroe. He nodded to indicate that the time was agreeable. He had come to Cairo shortly after Jim had left the country. Now he looked at Jim and cleared his throat as if wanting to say something but knowing he must choose his words carefully. After a pause he said tentatively, "I heard a good deal about you when I first came and I've heard a good deal since you got back."

"But very little that was good," Jim said. "Nothing good about my father's wife, either, probably."

"I wanted to speak to you about that situation," Monroe said. "I tried to do something about it, but I could not. Your father, as I'm sure you know, was a strong-minded man. The trouble was everything he said and did made it worse."

"I suppose that's why he's hated now."

Monroe nodded. "That's part of it. What the

bank did before his death is the rest of it." He cleared his throat again. "I've been wanting to talk to you, Mr. Dunn. I can understand how you might feel vindictive about this whole situation. It could conceivably be worse with your . . . your . . . step-mother. What I'm trying to say is that every man who belongs to the band of which I am the shepherd is in debt to the bank. I hope that you and Mrs. Dunn will find it in your hearts to be generous."

"That's up to Judge Riddle," Jim said, and rose.

Monroe, too, got to his feet. "Just one thing more. Would it help if I went out to talk to Mrs. Dunn?"

"I doubt it," Jim said. "Why should it?"

"I don't know, except that Mrs. Dunn seemed like a bigger and finer woman than some who criticize her. I would have gone long ago if I had thought it would do any good, but I didn't know how I would be received." He paused, and when Jim reached the front door, he asked, "What are your plans, Mr. Dunn?"

"Bury Lennie," Jim said, "and then get the men who killed him."

Jim expected him to say that he should leave it in the hands of the sheriff, or that vengeance was the Lord's, but he simply nodded, and said, "I understand."

Jim drove on to Main Street and tied the team in front of Doc Finley's place. Finley was not in his office. Probably down at Rafferty's getting his eye opener, Jim thought, so he climbed the stairs to Judge Riddle's office over the bank. Riddle rose at once and held out his hand, saying, "Glad to see you, boy. I was figuring on going out to the Box D this afternoon."

"You'll be there anyhow," Jim said, and told him about Lennie.

Riddle sat there in silence for a long time, his face supported by the tips of his fingers. Finally he said, "I'm sorry, Jim. Lennie was a good man." He was silent again, then he said, "Well, it won't do any good to tell Watrous. He'll ask if you recognized any of them, or their horses. When you say no, he'll say you don't have any proof as to who did the killing."

"I didn't aim to tell Watrous," Jim said. "I'll do my own snake stomping."

"Sure, you've got to," the Judge said. "Funny thing, me telling you that when all these years I've argued that the law must be enforced by duly elected officers. But you're in for trouble, Jim. A lot of folks think you shot Monte Smith. Now they're blaming you for Frank Castleman s disappearance."

Surprised, Jim said, "I didn't know he had disappeared."

"He did, slick as a whistle. Just didn't show up for work yesterday morning, so Bill Royal went down to his house. His horse was gone. Bed hadn't been slept in. Wasn't any sign of a fight or anything. Looked like he just rode off and didn't come back."

"Chances are he was riding with Colter yesterday," Jim said.

"Maybe. Maybe not. He's a queer one. Not like Colter at all." Riddle motioned as if to push Castleman aside. "This bank business was what I wanted to see you about, Jim. I can go ahead and decide things since I'm administrator of the estate. Doc and Fred Hines own a small part of the bank, but of course Sherm had the controlling interest. He trusted Fred who has been cashier for years, and since Sherm's death, I've left everything of a minor nature in his hands. But now we're faced with a decision of major policy. A lot of notes are coming due this fall. Other people are behind in their interest. To save trouble later when the estate is settled, I think you and Mrs. Dunn had better talk this over with me and Doc and Fred."

Jim rolled a cigarette, thinking how often he had run into this business of people owing the bank money since he had come back. He said, "When I left here, I thought Dad was pretty well respected. Now he's dead, and every man and his dog cusses him. Ann says he didn't do anything he didn't have to. He was just keeping the bank solvent."

Riddle got out a cigar and bit off the end. He pushed himself up out of his chair and walked to a window that looked down into Cairo's Main Street, dragging his heavy, built-up shoe with each step of his left leg. He put his cigar into his mouth and turned to Jim.

"I don't know," Riddle said. "I don't know what I'd have done if I'd been in Sherm's boots and had the responsibility he had. Pretty easy to criticize, standing on the fringe and watching Sherm who was in the middle." He paused, chewing on his cigar, and then asked, "What's she like, Jim? Really like?"

He put his cigarette out, puzzled by this question which seemed to have no relationship to what they had been talking about. He said, "You told me she had the face of an angel, but maybe she was a devil in disguise. I'm still not sure, Judge, but she sure pulls on a man. And Maggie likes her. Pretty hard to fool Maggie."

Riddle struck a match and drew on his cigar. When he had it fired properly, he dropped the match into the spittoon. He said, "When you left three years ago, I couldn't talk to you, Jim. I think I can now. It's why I said in the note I sent you that we needed you. What we do with the bank is going to decide the life and happiness of almost every man in the valley. I'm speaking literally when I say life. We can take advantage of the times and close out all the farmers and ranchers who can't meet their obligations. If we do, we'll have men shooting themselves or going to hell in one way or another."

Riddle returned to his chair and sat down. "I

worked with Sherm time and time again. We built the town. We financed the irrigation project that puts water on Ruby Mesa." He spread his hands. "Hell, I could go on like that for an hour, but you know how it was. What I'm trying to say is that we got along right up till the last. It seemed to me he was just too damned hard on some of the boys, but like I said, I don't know what I'd have done if I'd been in his place."

"How much of this was due to Ann?"

"I don't know, but I always had the notion that Sherm got tougher after the women in town snubbed Ann." Riddle tapped his fingers on the desk. "I'm afraid she'll want to operate like Sherm did. That's the help I expect from you. I think we've got to be more lenient. I hope you can make Ann see it that way."

"According to the will, we're all tied up for another six months? I mean, we can't say the ranch belongs to me and the bank to Ann?"

"No, we can't," Riddle answered. "If you die, everything goes to Ann. If she dies, everything goes to you."

"Meanwhile you have to run the bank?"

"Well yes, but I don't want to make the decision by myself. After all, you and Ann are the ones who inherit, so the bank should be operated by policy that you two agree on."

"I've got my say about the bank at least until the estate is settled?"

"That's right," Riddle agreed, "but let me add one other thing before you make your decision. You've got two things to overcome, the reputation you had when you went away, and the sour taste Sherm left in everybody's mouth when he died. I don't think it's too much to say that what you decide will determine your future here."

"What if Ann and I don't agree?"

"I guess we'll just have to rock along," Riddle said, "and be pretty tough on the boys who are behind."

The Judge didn't say it in words, but Jim sensed what was in his mind. If he authorized Fred Harris to be lenient and the bank went under, he might be held responsible, and he didn't have the courage to take that chance.

It all added up to about the same answer, Jim told himself. What the Judge was saying now, the preacher's request that he be generous, what Rafferty had said the first night he was in Cairo, the bitterness that was an acid in Bill Royal's veins. Make up for Sherman Dunn's tough policy. Love those who hate you and kick you in the teeth. But why should he? What did he, Jim Dunn, owe any of them? What help would he get in his fight with Bud Colter?

"To hell with them, Judge," Jim rose, restless, and wanting no more of this talk. "They've had me black-balled ever since I got back, all but you and Doc and Rafferty. Anyhow, I've got Lennie to

172

bury and some coyotes to hunt."

"I wouldn't ask you to put off the burying," Riddle said. "As for the coyote hunting, a few hours won't hurt. Will you bring Ann to town first thing in the morning? We'll meet in the back room of the bank. I'll have Doc and Fred Hines there."

Tomorrow morning when he should be out hunting Bud Colter. One man against five, or six if Castleman had joined up with them. He had no one to side him, no one except Alec and Sugar, both so stove up they wouldn't be able to fork a horse for a week. He could wait until Luke Dilly got here with his three men, but that would be putting it off two more days, and those hours might make all the difference in the world for Box D.

Then an idea struck him and he laughed. "All right, Judge. You get some help for me when I go after Colter, and I'll do it."

He wheeled and strode to the door. There he stopped, for Ginny was coming up the stairs. She did not see him until she was on the landing, then he reached for her and brought her to him and kissed her. For a moment she seemed too shocked to do anything; she was limp in his arms, giving him nothing, then he let her go and she backed into her father's office, her eyes wide and filled with misery.

"Jim, I didn't want you to go out there," she said. "Twice I begged you not to, in our house and in front of Rafferty's, but you went."

This made no sense to Jim. He followed her into her father's office, glancing at the Judge who now seemed to lack the great strength Jim had always associated with him just as he had with his father. Riddle shook his head, plainly unhappy and troubled.

Jim pinned his gaze on Ginny's face. He said, "I don't get this. I wasn't much when I left here, but I'm not the same man now. You must know that. Your dad does."

"Please, Jim," she said in a low voice.

"I've got a right to know what's wrong. I'm going to make something out of myself and out of the Box D, but . . ."

"Jim." Riddle was on his feet, bending forward, his big palms down on his desk. "Colter came into Rafferty's the night after you whipped him and talked. He linked your name with Ann's."

"And you told Ginny?"

"No. She heard it the next morning from Mrs. Hofferd and Mrs. Royal."

He looked at Ginny and shook his head. Maybe she belonged in this town, listening to its lies and gossips. For three years he had loved a Ginny Riddle he had built in his mind, but not the real Ginny. He wheeled and started toward the door.

"Jim, Jim," she cried and ran after him and grabbed his arm. "Marry me, Jim. Don't wait. Don't put it off. I'm afraid to wait."

"I asked you to wait six months," he said evenly.

"I didn't think it was unreasonable then and I don't now."

He jerked free from her grip and left the office. He found Doc Finley in, shook hands with him, and asked for a coffin. They loaded it into the back of the wagon and he drove out of town. He saw Bill Royal on the street. Shep Hofferd. Herman Bloch, the blacksmith.

They stared at him as if he were a complete stranger, but he wasn't. He was Sherman Dunn's son, the Sherman Dunn who had helped start this town and owned the bank they had been so willing to borrow from and hated now that it was time to repay the loans, the Sherman Dunn who had been generous many times. But as Rafferty said, they would forget everything except how it had been just before Sherman Dunn's death.

The wind that rushed down the valley was biting with cold; the sky was menacingly gray. But Jim, buried in the deep pit of his thoughts was not aware of either.

CHAPTER XVI

They buried Lennie Nolan in the tightly fenced, little graveyard at the foot of the south mesa hill, the sky so forbidding and the light so thin that it seemed like evening at three o'clock on this afternoon in late October. Three other Box D hands were buried here. Jim's older brother who had died when he was a baby. Jim's mother. All of these were old, grass-covered graves that had been here for years. Jim remembered them well, all except the one marked "Sherman Dunn" that lacked the heavy grass covering.

No one had told Jim about his father's funeral, but he could imagine how it had been, burying a man like Sherman Dunn, as if the stars and moon and the sun had been swept out of the sky. And all the time Bud Colter was standing here, looking sad but feeling fine inside, for he would be thinking ahead to the day when he'd be the husband of the woman who owned Box D.

Jim had gone over it in his mind many times, and that was the only way it made any sense. But Ann? He didn't think she had any part of it. She had nothing to gain. She was standing beside him now while the preacher droned on about the greatest thing in the world was the sacrifice Lennie had made, giving his life for a friend.

Now and then Jim looked at Ann, but she was not aware of his gaze. She was crying softly, a handkerchief over her eyes. Again Jim told himself she had nothing to do with the death of his father. He had given her the first peace and security she could remember, she had said. She would be a fool, then, to scheme with Colter to commit murder. Jim had not made up his mind yet whether she was good or bad, but he did know she wasn't a fool.

The preacher began to recite the Twenty-Third Psalm. Jim felt Ann's hand slip down his arm and grip his hand, and he looked across the grave at Ginny and knew she was watching. Ann had taken a proprietary attitude toward him from the first moment any of them had come. Maybe it was natural. In six months Box D would go to him, but now she was living here, she was Sherman Dunn's widow, so in reality they were Box D. Or what was left of it.

He thought of Lennie who had been a boy in his late teens when he had first come here. He had been a good, dependable hand right from the start, the kind you could put up there in the line cabin and be sure that no Box D cows were drifting over the divide. There had been nothing of the tumble-weed in Lennie Nolan. He had liked it here, he'd got along with Sherm and Luke Dilly, so he'd stayed.

Everyone in town knew him. Bill Royal. Shep Hofferd. Hank Watrous. Herman Bloch, the black-smith. Jim could go on down the list. But who had come to attend the funeral? Just the preacher, Doc Finley, Rafferty, the Judge, and Ginny.

The preacher was closing with the Lord's Prayer. Ann's crying was audible now and Jim put his arm around her. He didn't feel like crying. He was too numb, and he kept reaching ahead in his mind to the time when he would find Bud Colter. But there was the one thought around which all others bent and gave, like a great rock dividing the current of a river. If he had been the first to step out of the cabin, ahead of Lennie, he would be the one they were burying now.

Jim heard the preacher's "Amen." The coffin was lowered into the grave, and Alec and Rafferty picked up shovels. Jim turned Ann toward the house and Maggie came up on the other side of her and the three of them walked across the hay field, the others except Alec and Rafferty stringing along behind. A few small snowflakes floated before them in the wind, and Jim thought absently that Lennie had been right. The first October storm was here.

The preacher and Doc Finley came into the house, shook hands, and left. The Judge and Ginny lingered a moment. Ginny very stiff and proper, her gaze never quite meeting Jim's. Ann wasn't crying now, but she seemed unable to talk, and she stayed very close to Jim's side as if she found strength and comfort in his presence.

"Did you tell Mrs. Dunn about our meeting in the morning?" Riddle asked.

Jim shook his head. "We haven't talked about anything all day. Anyhow, I didn't say I'd be there."

"I think you will, Jim." Riddle leaned forward, putting his weight on his cane. "I don't want to bother you at a time like this, Mrs. Dunn, but there is one very important matter concerning the policy of the bank that must be discussed. I have put it off because Jim wasn't available, but now that he is here, we should discuss this matter with Fred Hines and Doc Finley."

"Of course we'll be there," Ann said.

Jim couldn't argue. Not this afternoon. Since it was something that had to be done sometime, it might as well be done in the morning, so he said, "All right, Judge."

Riddle nodded. He said, "Come on, Ginny," and hobbled to the door.

Jim walked across the yard with them to their buggy. He gave Ginny a hand up into the seat, then stepped back while Riddle climbed in and took the lines. Jim put a hand on the dashboard and leaned forward, his eyes searching Ginny's pale face. He asked, "Where do we stand, Ginny?"

He was instantly sorry he had asked. She said, "I think you stand very close to Ann Dunn." The pink tip of her tongue touched her dry lips, and she shivered. "I'm sorry I listened to that gossip we talked about this morning, but you're a man, and she's very lovely."

"And you're a fool," Riddle said sharply.

"No." Ginny shook her head. "Something's happening, Jim. I don't know what it is, but I feel it, like a storm coming."

Jim stepped back, his face rigidly masked

against his feelings. During all the years he had been gone, he had dreamed about Ginny, and loved her. He had mentally endowed her with a woman's good characteristics, but he had neglected to give her a woman's weaknesses. That she would be jealous of his father's widow was a possibility that had never occurred to him.

"We're all upset," Riddle said. "It's no time to talk about a thing like this."

Ginny was the one who leaned forward now, her wool cap pulled down over her blonde hair, her coat collar buttoned up under her chin. "Wait, Dad," she said. "Jim, I know I was wrong not to trust you. From now on I will. It's just that I've heard so much about her . . ."

"Which may all be lies," Riddle said. "I watched her when we buried Sherm, and I watched her again today. She's a good woman if I ever saw one, a damned sight better than the women in Cairo who gab about her."

"That may be," Ginny said. "What I want to say is this, Jim. I've waited for you for three years, not hearing from you or anything. If I've waited that long, I shouldn't have to wait another six months now that you're back."

She didn't know about Frank Castleman who had disappeared. About Bud Colter and his bunch of hardcases. He didn't think she'd understand if her told her. All she wanted was to get married. It was that simple to her.

But it was a man's world, a jungle where it was kill or be killed; there were the little men, the yapping, snarling curs like Bill Royal and Hank Watrous who did nothing more than snarl, and there were the dangerous, slinking wolves like Castleman and Colter, and men like Toy Severe who made a profession out of killing. He, Jim Dunn, had to fight them all. No, she wouldn't understand.

"I made a mistake asking you to wait," he said stiffly, and lifted his hat to her. "Good-by."

He swung around and walked into the house. Maggie had built a fire in the fireplace and he stood in front of it, cold all the way into his bones. Ann was nowhere around. Maggie was back in the kitchen getting supper.

Rafferty came in presently, puffing and blowing, and stood beside Jim at the fire. He said, "We'll miss Lennie, Jim. Every time Alec and Sugar come to town to get a drink, I'll look up and expect to see Lennie with 'em."

Jim nodded, not wanting to talk. Then Rafferty said, "There's a lot of feeling in town, Jim. I thought you ought to know. Royal's doing most of the talking since Castleman disappeared. He claims you killed Monte Smith and Castleman, and he's after Watrous to come and get you."

Jim looked at him, the one friend he had in town beside Riddle and Doc Finley. Suddenly the tension that had been building in him through these hours exploded into a string of oaths. He stopped only when he was out of breath. Then he said, "I'm sorry. Raff, seems like the bank has got everybody over a barrel: townsmen, farmers, little ranchers, everybody. Ann and me have got to decide how to treat 'em. This morning the preacher asked me to be generous. A little later the Judge said about the same thing. But why should I? If Colter showed up in town when I did, they'd back him, every one of 'em."

"Depends," Rafferty said. "But that ain't exactly the point. You'll go easy on 'em because you're a hell of a decent man, now that you've got your feet on the ground." He held out his hand. "So long, Jim."

Jim gripped his hand. "Thanks, Raff," he said, and watched Rafferty leave the house and get into his buggy and start for town.

That night Jim ate supper in the dining room with Ann and Maggie because Ann asked him. But it was not the way it had been before he'd left. He should have known it wouldn't be. A white tablecloth spread on the oak table, napkins, candles in tall, silver holders, plates with a marine landscape painted on them, so thin he was afraid they'd snap in two every time his fork or spoon touched them, thick brown gravy the way he liked it that must be spooned out of a tureen in the middle of the table.

No, it wasn't the way it had been, but he found himself liking it, and that was odd, never having lived in this fashion before. Now and then he looked across the table at Ann when he felt her eyes on him, and she gave him just a hint of a smile. Neither of them, he knew, was listening to Maggie's chatter.

When they were finished, she asked him to build a fire upstairs in her parlor. When it was going with a great snapping and leaping of flames up the chimney, she wanted the divan drawn up next to the fireplace. He sat down beside her because he felt a loneliness that had not been in him since he had returned, stemming, perhaps, from his strained relationship with Ginny. He sensed that Ann felt it, too. It must have been an old need in her. Except for Maggie, she had been alone for six months.

She sat very close to him, and after a moment reached out and took his hand that was next to her. "Jim, I hope you'll believe me when I tell you I think you're a wonderful man. It wouldn't mean much to say that if I hadn't heard what a no-good boy you were when you left."

"It's like I told you the first time I saw you," he said. "I've been purified in hell."

"Yes, but if it hadn't been in you when you left, it wouldn't have come out," she said quickly. "I've heard Maggie say that. Sherm, too. He never really worried about you. He just kept hoping you'd come back."

He was silent, feeling the point of her shoulder

against his, her soft hand over his big-knuckled one, then he said the words he had been wanting to say to her for a long time. "I was wrong raising the row I did with Dad. If I'd known you, it would have been different."

"Ah, Jim, Jim," she said. "I told you that most people liked me after they knew me. There's something else you don't understand about yourself. I was sure of it after hearing Sherm talk, and knowing you now, I'm more sure of it. You were so much like Sherm that you didn't get along. I think it was because he didn't give you any real responsibility here on the ranch, so you took it out in the drinking and fighting that people seem to remember about you."

He nodded. "I guess that's right. I hadn't thought of it much except that when I got away from Dad, I changed."

"That proves it," she said. "And you're going to be a solid rock that will hold this entire valley steady just like Sherm was."

"I don't know," he said. "Right now I feel like kicking the whole bunch into the Uncompahgre."

"I know how you feel," she said. "But I can forgive them because I'm bigger than they are. That's what makes them so mad. It's always that way, Jim. People who don't have anything hate the ones who do and they're afraid of them. That's why they feel about Sherm like they do. But if he'd let those loans go on and on, and the bank had gone broke, like a lot of them have around here, how would they feel?"

He nodded. "A man's wrong either way he jumps. That's what the Judge wants to see us about in the morning. It's a policy meeting, he calls it. We close everyone out that we can and not take any chances, or give Fred Hines his head so he can use his own judgment."

She looked at him as if wondering which way he would vote. She said, "Jim, we've got to leave it to Fred. Sherm trusted him. Banking is his business, not yours or mine or Riddle's. The truth is that what the bank did when Sherm was alive was on Fred's advice. People in town don't know that, so they blame Sherm."

He shook his head. "I'll keep thinking on it, but, there's something funny about Cairo."

"You'll change the town in time," she said. "It'll grow. New men will come in. Young men who'll see things the way you do."

The fire began to die down. He rose and threw a piece of pine on it and walked to the window. He couldn't tell whether it was snowing in earnest yet or not. Ann, still on the divan, said, "Jim, do you know how old I am?"

"Thirty-five," he said.

"That's what Sherm thought," she said. "Colter thinks so, too. It was better that Sherm believed it because he wouldn't have married me if I'd been too young. I'm twenty-five. I can prove it if it's

185

necessary. I ran away from home when I was four-teen. I'll tell you about it someday if you want to know. Actually I was grown then, as big as I am now, and I looked much older than I was. I had to say I was twenty-four to get a job. People believed me."

He didn't, but there was no use to tell her. She rose and came to him. "Jim, you talk about being purified in hell. So was I, right up until I married Sherm. That's why it's been so wonderful to live here, and be safe and protected and live the way I wanted to."

She was looking at him, her face alive and eager, her full red lips moist and parted just a little. She was breathing hard now, and her hands clutched his arms. "Jim, would it be wrong to love the son of the man you had been married to? I know what people would say, but they're saying it anyway. All I want to know is what you think."

He thought of Ginny and what she had said about Ann and how that she had not trusted him because he was a man. He shook his head, not sure he had lost Ginny, but certain that this would not work.

"I love Ginny," he said.

"Oh, not her," Ann cried. "Not that . . ." She stopped. "Jim, I've pushed too hard, haven't I? And you probably think I'm lying about my age. Will you give me a week, Jim? I'll write to the town where I was born . . ."

The window snapped in front of them, a hornet

186

buzzed past, and something went *thwack* into the opposite wall. He was dragging her down as the sound of the shot came to them. "Stay out of the light," he shouted at her, and crawling to the door, plunged through it and along the hall and down the stairs.

He grabbed a rifle off the antlers beside the door and ran outside. He could hear the steady beat of hoofs on frozen ground as a horse fled down valley. Alec and Sugar ran toward him, Alec bawling, "Who the hell fired that shot?"

"Colter, I reckon," Jim said. "I'll stay up until midnight, Alec, then I'll wake you and you can get Sugar up about three. Tomorrow I'm going hunting."

He went back into the house, found his father's sheepskin, put on his hat and came back. He was sure Colter would not return, but he could not afford to take any chances. Could it have been Castleman? Well, what difference did it make? Both wanted to kill him, both were capable of bushwhacking him. They had proved that.

But there was one difference. Colter wanted Ann. Now Jim mentally began putting everything in place at the window, Ann's upturned face very close to his, the lamp behind them, and Colter watching, out there far enough so the scene had been lighted and framed for him. No, it must have been Colter, still hoping, still trying to make his plans work out.

Tomorrow Jim would be the hunter, for it was better, even with the odds against him, to be the hunter instead of the hunted. If he waited long enough, sooner or later Colter would succeed. Then, against his will, Jim's thoughts turned to Ann, and the problem that her presence here made for him. He pondered this as he paced along the cottonwoods toward the barn, tiny flakes of snow biting at his face, but no answer came to him.

Chapter XVII

For an hour Bud Colter stood in the dark beside his horse, his eyes on the Box D ranch house. There were lights in the front room and upstairs in Ann's parlor. Sooner or later Jim Dunn was bound to appear at one of the windows, long enough for Colter to get a shot at him. Or so he hoped, but the minutes dragged out and he caught only an occasional glimpse of his man. There was nothing for Colter to do but think, while the cold worked into the very marrow of his bones.

Looking back over these past hours, it was hard for him to believe that his world had tumbled down on his head as it had. Time after time he had ridden these hills, or reined up on some high ridge and looked down over this valley, and dreamed the dreams of an owner.

He had never anticipated any trouble. Sure, he knew Sherm had a boy, but it never occurred to him that this Jim Dunn would turn out to be the tough fighting man that he was. So Colter had mentally brushed him aside, telling himself that young Dunn could be disposed of as easily as his father had been.

The worst mistake he had made was to take Ann for granted. He was sure she had married Sherm strictly for his money which would go to her when he was dead, and that was what Ann had wanted as long as he had known her. Colter had been careful as long as Sherm was alive, but after his death there were business matters to talk to Ann about, so he had spent a good deal of time with Ann in her private parlor because that was where she liked to be.

Colter had always assumed Ann loved him. Many woman had. Why should Ann be any different? Now, looking back, he could not remember a single time that she had shown any passion when he had kissed her. He had never doubted she would marry him when she had the opportunity. So he had gone on making his plans and dreaming his dreams, and turning out to be a damn fool.

He saw it plain enough now. She was chasing young Dunn for all she was worth. All this time she had been playing it cagey, holding Colter off while she waited to find out what Jim Dunn was like. If he had never come back, she would eventually have married Colter, but he had come back, and he was the kind of man she wanted.

So he waited, with an occasional snowflake coming in on the wind and stinging his face, and he wondered how it was possible that Jim Dunn could have had so much good luck while he, Bud Colter, had so much that was bad. Take Castleman that first night. He had no reason to miss. Or the fight Colter had had with Dunn. The bastard got in a few lucky punches and whipped him. He could never do it again. If Colter had won, he'd have killed Dunn right there in the bunkhouse. He'd have killed Alec, too, and that simple-minded Watrous would have believed any story he told.

Or the business up there at the line cabin. If Ash Mason hadn't been so jumpy and drilled Lennie Nolan before Dunn stepped out of the cabin, they could have got both of them. Or if Dunn hadn't been so stubborn and stayed inside the cabin, they'd have got him. Then somebody had jumped into the fight, probably old Sugar and Alec, and one of them had been lucky enough to shoot Del Mason through the head. Ash hadn't been worth a damn since. He wouldn't help Colter and Lannigen chase Dunn down the mountain. Dunn had been lucky there, too. His horse was fresh and theirs were tired, so he'd got away.

A man can be lucky just so long. In cards or anything else, luck ran in chunks, and sooner or later it was bound to reverse itself. The trick was to hang on until it did. That was why he was out here tonight.

He didn't have much more time if he was going to have any help. There were increasing signs that Toy Severe was about to take over, and Lannigen and Ash Mason would go along. They'd hit the bank and be gone one of these days, and there wasn't a single damn thing he could do about it.

He'd made a mistake fetching Castleman out here. He had thought Castleman would help him get Dunn, but they'd handled the man wrong. He was mule stubborn. If they gave him a gun, he'd clean up the bunch of them. He'd said that over and over. He was crazy. Apparently he hated Colter and the others more than he hated Jim Dunn.

Suddenly Colter was aware that Dunn was standing at a window in Ann's parlor. His heart began to pound as he raised the rifle to his shoulder. This was what he had been waiting for. But now he was so cold he was shivering and his eyes were filled with tears. He lowered the rifle and rubbed his eyes, and when he looked again, both Ann and Dunn were at the window.

Warm and cozy, Colter thought bitterly, with a fire in the fireplace. Dunn had been making love to her, and she'd be willing. Why, she'd have him married to her in a week. He raised the rifle again, still trembling, but it was not from the cold as much as the rage that swept through him. He didn't care which one he shot. She had it coming as much as Dunn.

Colter eared the hammer back, but now that the moment was actually here, it was Dunn's head he took the bead on. He fired. Both heads disappeared, but whether he had scored a hit or not he didn't know. He swung into the saddle, jammed the Winchester into the scabbard, and headed down valley. He slowed up before he had gone half a mile, realizing there was no hurry. Colter didn't expect to be chased. Dunn would get a crew together as soon as he could and start combing the country, but until he was able to round up a bunch of men as salty as he was, Colter was reasonably sure he'd stick close to the ranch. Dunn had got more out of Alec and old Sugar already than Colter had ever thought he would.

He reached the point where the trail to Monument Rock left the valley when he heard horses coming down. He pulled up, uncertain about this. His men should be at the cabin. He'd seen Dunn at the window, so it couldn't be him. That left one slim possibility. Hank Watrous might have gathered a posse and was out after them, if Dunn had made Watrous believe Colter was responsible for Lennie Nolan's death. He discarded the idea at once. Watrous wouldn't leave Cairo, especially on a cold night like this.

So he waited, his gun in his hand, while the horses came down the rocky trail to the valley. He wasn't sure how many, three or four, then he heard one of the men say something. Toy Severe's voice! So that was it. They had made their plans, Severe and Lannigen and Ash Mason, and they had dealt him out.

Colter's first reaction was to hell with them. Let them go past and he'd hang out in the cabin until he learned whether he'd put a bullet through Jim Dunn's head or not. As far as he was concerned, that was the only important thing.

By the time they were abreast of him, he had changed his mind. Dunn wasn't going anywhere. If Colter had to do the job by himself, and it looked like he would, he could attend to it a week from now as well as tomorrow. On the other hand, Severe and the rest might be planning to knock the bank over in the morning. He'd better go along if he wanted a cut of the money. Right now it looked as if that was all he'd get. So he called, "That you, Toy?"

"Well, so you're on your way back," Severe said. "We didn't expect you till morning."

"Where you headed?"

"Town," Severe said coolly. "We made a little change, Bud. I'm giving the orders now. Any objections?"

They were not far apart, but the night was so dark that Colter could make out only a vague shape that was Severe and his horse. He couldn't be sure of the other men's location except for the glow of a cigarette in the mouth of one of them. He felt certain Severe had a gun in his hand, and he'd shoot if the answer he heard didn't sound right.

"No objections," Colter said mildly, "except that I'd like to know what's going on."

"We're taking the bank in the morning," Severe said, "and then we're hitting out for Utah. We're tired of waiting for you to make good on your fat promises."

"You damned betcha we are," Ash Mason said in a surly voice.

He had been sullen from the time his brother had been killed, Colter thought, sullen and unpredictable and therefore dangerous. "Well," Colter said, "you could use another man. I didn't figure you boys would cut me out like this."

"Sure, we could use you," Severe said. "Only thing is you've got a one-track mind, wanting to plug Dunn. We can't see no profit in that, the way things are shaping up."

"Maybe not," Colter said. "I'll ride along." He swung in beside Severe. "Where's Castleman?"

"Behind," Severe said casually. "Riding face-down across his horse. He kept nagging me to get him some grub, so I done it and untied his hands to let him eat. Then, by God, he threw the whole mess into my face." He paused, and added indifferently, "When I got the stuff clawed out of my eyes so I could see, I plugged him."

The casual way Severe told it sent a chill down Colter's back. Severe was like that. When the mood was on him, he would shoot a man with as little concern as a butcher would beef a steer. Perhaps these last few days had been as hard on the little gunman as they had on Colter and Ash Mason. Cooped up in the cabin because he had been afraid Dunn would notify the Texas authorities, and having to guard Frank Castleman, had finally brought him to the exploding point.

Colter thought it over, not wanting to irritate him, but puzzled by his reason for bringing the body along. He didn't understand, either, why Severe was showing himself in town now. He said, "Thought you were going to stay out of sight, Toy?"

"I'll take a chance on being seen for what's in the bank," Severe said. "Main thing was we didn't want to ride to town in the morning and have tired horses before we done the job."

"What are you aiming to do with Castleman's carcass?"

"Leave it in front of Watrous' house," Severe said. "We figured Watrous wouldn't find it till morning. He'll think Jim Dunn plugged Castleman. I'm guessing Watrous will get a posse together and go after Dunn. While they're gone, we clean the bank out. How does it sound?"

This was probably Severe's idea right down the line, but there was at least one thing wrong with it. Colter said, "Fine, except that Dunn will probably

195

fetch Ann to town in the morning to shop. She's been doing it every Saturday."

It had been a gesture of defiance on her part toward the women of Cairo more than any need to buy. She might drive to town with Maggie, but Colter didn't mention that possibility. Severe was silent as they climbed the hill to Ruby Mesa, Colter dropping behind Severe.

No lights were showing anywhere around Box D. Colter wished fretfully that there was some way he could find out whether he had killed Dunn or not. He had probably failed, or there would be lights around the house, and Alec Torrin would likely be on his way to town to get Watrous and Doc Finley. No, he must have failed again.

They reached the top and Colter touched steel to his horse and came abreast of Severe. The gunman said, "Hell, I didn't think about Dunn coming to town in the morning."

"There might be another way." Colter's heart began to race as the possibilities of a new idea began working in his mind. "Toy, you know that bastard has got the Injun sign on me. Nothing I try seems to work."

"We've noticed that," Severe said scornfully. "The great Bud Colter rodding Box D was one man, but the Bud Colter who took a hell of a whipping from Dunn and has been jumping around ever since like a grasshopper in a hot skillet is something else."

What Severe said was so true that it made Colter furious, but right now he couldn't afford to be furious. So he held his tongue until he was able to say with proper humility, "Yeah, my luck's sure been sour. Well, what I was wondering is whether you're faster'n Dunn."

Severe was insulted. "You're damn right I am. Why?"

"Well, there's your answer. If Dunn shows up in town in the morning, you jump him on the street. Give him an even chance and nobody will blame you. Hell, everybody knows he fired us for no reason. We've got plenty of cause to plug him. While the excitement's going on, the rest of us will take care of the bank."

"And let you double-cross me?" Severe cried. "I'm not that soft between the ears."

"I couldn't unless Ash and Crip did," Colter said. "Seems like you ought to trust them."

"Sure, sure," Severe said hastily.

"Think it over," Colter went on. "You'd have every man in town out there on Main Street shaking your hand. You could take some time with Watrous, asking him if he was going to hold you and so on. Won't take us more'n three, four minutes in the bank. We'll leave our horses in the alley. There's a back door that opens into a hall. Ever been back there?"

"No."

"Well, from the back door you can go up the

stairs to Riddle's and Flanders' offices, or follow the hall into the bank. The hall goes past a room Hines uses for a private office. Soon as the shooting starts, Hines will be in the street. That'll just leave young Buckley in the bank. He might run out, too. Give us, well, not more'n five minutes and then all you've got to do is to catch us on the bridge."

To Colter's surprise, Ash Mason said, "Sounds good to me, Toy. I dunno who plugged Del, but I'll feel better when I know Dunn's cashed in."

"Yeah, might work," Severe said thoughtfully. "If I get held up, you boys can wait for me at the line cabin. We figured on picking up some grub there anyhow." He yawned. "Well, there's Cairo. I'll be ready to roll in soon as I get a drink at Rafferty's."

They rode in silence then, and for the first time in days a deep sense of satisfaction eased Colter's taut nerves. He pictured Jim Dunn lying in the street with a bullet hole in his head. There would be snow on the ground in the morning. Maybe a little blood on the snow. Red blood on white snow! It would be a pretty sight if it was Dunn's blood.

For a moment the wish was in his mind that it would be his bullet which would make the hole in Dunn's head, but only for a moment. Let Severe take the risk. After all, what difference did it make whose bullet it was?

CHAPTER XVIII

Hank Watrous had done a man's work from the time he'd been big enough to drive a team, putting the lines around his waist and gripping the plow handles on both sides of him. He could not remember when he'd had enough sleep. He'd got up day after day before the sun was up, winter and summer, working every daylight hour, and then doing chores by lantern light, but he'd been saddled by debt from the time he'd struck out for himself. Whatever profit had come to him for his labor had not lingered in his hands, but had gone to the bank for interest. Then, when money had tightened up, the bank had taken everything.

Watrous, with no knowledge of economics, had little understanding of what was happening all over the country. He simply hated Wall Street, banks and bankers, and he hated Jim Dunn because he was the son of a man who had owned the controlling interest in the Cairo bank and would probably own it himself when the estate was settled.

To make it worse, he had not even had a reasonable part of a night's sleep all week. He had been up one entire night because he'd gone far back into the adobe hills and brought Orie Mann to town and jailed him. The next night Jim Dunn had come to town, Monte Smith was shot and killed, Frank Castleman had disappeared, Lennie Nolan was killed, and his baby had the colic. All of these things, including the colic, Watrous blamed on Dunn.

So, when his wife shook him awake on this bleak Saturday morning in late October and screamed that there was a dead man in front of the house, he grunted, "Dunn" and turned over. But his wife wouldn't stand for him going back to sleep again, so she kept on shaking him as she screamed, "Hank, there's a dead man on a horse in front of the house. You've got to get up and do something."

He rubbed his eyes and told himself if Jim Dunn was out there, his troubles were over. He pulled on his slippers, and clad only in his undershirt and drawers, plodded to the front window. A horse was tied to a lilac bush in the front yard. The man draped across the saddle looked dead enough. Watrous couldn't tell from the house who it was. Then he looked at the horse again. It was Frank Castleman's black gelding. The dead man must be Castleman, and Jim Dunn must have shot him.

Watrous returned to his bedroom and dressed, then he buckled his gun belt around him, put on his sheepskin, and went into the kitchen. "I'll be back for breakfast," he said. "I'll have to take the body down to Doc Finley."

The baby sat in his high chair banging a spoon on the tray, looking better than he had all week. Mrs. Watrous, wearing a faded robe over her nightgown, stood at the stove stirring a pan of mush. Her hair, light brown but threaded with gray, hung down her back in a single braid. She was too tired to say or do anything she didn't have to. She simply nodded and went on stirring the mush.

Watrous left the house, thinking bleakly that she did not realize what had happened. All week she had been as upset as he had. At least twice each day she had said, "Don't you go sashaying off after nobody. Let these men kill themselves off. Don't you get yourself killed and leave me with three children."

One glance at the dead man showed Watrous it was Castleman. He untied the horse and led him down the street. He had not been Castleman's friend. No one had been the man's friend unless it was Bud Colter who had apparently left the country. Or maybe Bill Royal who got two men's work out of him for one man's wages. But the bank had taken Castleman's ranch, and for that reason Watrous felt a certain kinship with him.

All week Watrous had been putting off doing anything, although both Judge Riddle and Doc Finley had used their tongues harshly on him after they'd heard about Lennie Nolan's death. They'd said it was Bud Colter and it was up to Watrous to fetch him in, and he'd countered by asking how they knew it was Colter. On the other hand, Bill Royal and Shep Hofferd and their clique had been on his neck about Monte Smith's murder. Sure it was Jim Dunn, they'd said, and he'd asked the usual question. If there was any proof, he'd go after Dunn.

Now there could be no putting it off. He'd be glad to lock Dunn in jail, or see him dead if it came to a fight. But he had no idea how many townsmen he could persuade to make up a posse. Even if he had enough men, it wouldn't be easy. Dunn would certainly resist arrest. He'd have Alec Torrin and Sugar Sanders to help him fight. Maggie O'Boyle, too. She would be as good as any man. No, this was going to be tough and he dreaded telling his wife about it.

He was buried so deeply in his thoughts that he did not realize he had reached the Mercantile until Bill Royal, who had been sweeping off the porch, called to him, "Who is it this time?"

"Castleman," Watrous answered.

Royal swore. "I expected it. Who shot him, Dunn?"

"I reckon."

Shep Hofferd, standing in front of his livery stable, shouted, "You know it was Dunn."

"I ain't augering," Watrous said.

"What are you gonna do, sit on your behind until that bastard shoots every man in the county he don't like?"

"No, we're going after him," Watrous said. "You're riding with the posse."

"The hell I am," Hofferd said as if the idea was unreasonable. "I can't leave town. I run this stable by myself."

"You wanted action," Watrous said. "You're gonna get it. You'll ride, or I'll slap you into jail for being an accessory after the fact."

He wasn't sure what it meant, but he'd heard the expression somewhere and had liked it. It was enough to silence Hofferd who glared at Watrous, then turned on his heel and went into the stable. The liveryman was like everybody else, Watrous thought sourly. They cussed him for not doing his job. He could take the chances, they said. He got paid for it. But when it came to backing him up, there wasn't a man in town who'd do his part.

He led the black around to the alley and pounded on Doc Finley's back door. It was a good three minutes before Finley opened up, rubbing his eyes and wearing a long, cotton nightgown. "Damned funny when a man can't sleep on a morning . . ."

"Frank Castleman's been murdered," Watrous said.

Finley straightened and stopped rubbing his eyes. "Fetch him in," he said. "I'll get dressed."

Watrous untied the body, and carrying it into Finley's back room, laid it on a table. He waited until Finley came in, yawning and buttoning his shirt. "Two bullet holes in his belly," Finley said. "Fired from close up, too." He raised his head to look at Watrous. "Who do you figure did it, Hank?"

"Dunn."

"I thought you'd say that," Finley said. "Well, you're wrong, and you can tell Bill Royal and the rest of 'em they're wrong. If Dunn fired those shots, how did Castleman come to let him get close enough so he'd have those powder burns?"

Watrous didn't attempt to answer. He walked out of Finley's office. He had enough to worry about without having to figure out how Castleman got powder burns on him. And how the horse with Castleman's body on it happened to be tied in front of his house. Finley hadn't asked the question, but he would have if he'd known where Watrous found the body. It was a puzzler, all right, Watrous thought as he led the black gelding into the livery stable, but there wasn't anybody except Dunn who hated Castleman enough to shoot him.

"Far as I know, Frank didn't have no relatives," Watrous told Hofferd. "You'll have to see Judge Riddle about what to do with this animal." He walked out, calling back, "I'm going home to eat breakfast. We'll be riding in about an hour."

He ate his bowl of oatmeal mush and drank two cups of coffee and rose. "I'll be out of town this morning, Laura," he said. "I've got to go after Jim Dunn."

She screamed and grabbed him by the arm. "That outlaw will kill you. I knew this was going to happen as soon as I heard he was back. You can't go, Hank. You just can't go."

"Dunn ain't really an outlaw," he said. "Maybe he won't make no trouble."

But she was still clinging to him and crying, and suddenly he was out of patience with her. He hadn't been very proud of himself all week. A man should have a wife who would give him courage, not drain what little he had out of him. He took her by both shoulders and shoved her back until she had to give up her grip on his arms.

"Now listen, Laura," he said. "We've had purty tough times ever since we were married, but I've got a good job and I'd like to keep it. For the first time we've got a decent roof over our heads and enough grub to put in our bellies. Don't forget that."

He walked out through the back door, leaving her standing by the table crying softly, the baby still sitting in his high chair and banging the tray with his spoon. Watrous saddled his horse, went around by the courthouse to pick up a rifle from his office, and then rode on into Main Street and dismounted in front of Rafferty's.

It was still early, but he thought the news of Castleman's death would get around and there would be a crowd in the saloon. He was right. Almost every man in town was there except the preacher, Judge Riddle, and Fred Hines. He was most surprised at the presence of Bud Colter and his crew who were standing at the far end of the bar. But there were only four. It took a moment for him to figure out that Del Mason was not among them.

As Watrous came in, someone said. "Well, here's the great tin star."

That did it. The pressure that had been put on him this week, the accusations of cowardice, the threats that he'd never get another term: all of it piled up and boiled over. He walked along the row of men standing at the bar, not sure who had said it until he came to Alf Logan, the big, pimple-faced kid who drove Royal's delivery wagon.

Watrous grabbed him by the shoulder and yanked him away from the bar, he whirled the kid around and kicked him in the seat of the pants and Logan went flat on his face. For a moment he floundered there on the floor trying to get to his feet and failing, and when he finally succeeded, he went out of the saloon on the run.

"Hey, man," Rafferty said. "You must have a private bottle. I don't sell anything that'd make you do that."

"No bottle," Watrous said savagely. "I just ain't standing for no more guff from any of you. Now then." He backed up so he could see all the men except Colter and his bunch at the end of the bar. He had supposed they'd left the country, and it puzzled and bothered him that they were still here.

Watrous licked his lips and went on, "There's been a lot of squawking about the way I've done my job this week. All right, there ain't gonna be any more. You all know Frank Castleman was murdered and that I found his body this morning. I reckon there ain't much question about who done it. We're going after Jim Dunn this morning, and you boys that have done most of the squawking are making up the posse. Hofferd. Royal. Bloch. Flanders. Jessup. Go get your guns. Put on your heavy coats and fetch your horses. Fifteen minutes ought to do it."

"Now wait a minute," Doc Finley shouted. "You're going off half-cocked again. You don't have the slightest proof Jim did it."

"The hell we don't," Bill Royal said. "There's been trouble ever since he got to town. Before that we hadn't had any trouble clean back to the time he left three years ago. Now we've had enough and we're going after him."

"Wait. Wait now." Finley motioned to Watrous. "No use going out there after him. He's coming to town this morning with Mrs. Dunn. They ought to be here any minute. The Judge asked them to come to the bank . . ."

"All right, Doc," Watrous said. "It'll save us a cold ride. Shep. Bill." He pointed a forefinger at Hofferd and then at Royal. "Get your guns. I'm deputizing both of you to help me make the arrest as soon as Dunn gets to town."

They left the saloon, not giving Watrous any argument which surprised him. Then he was aware that Toy Severe was walking up to him and he turned toward the little gunman. He'd had very little to do with Severe and he hadn't wanted to. The man had remained in the background ever since he had started riding for the Box D, seldom even coming to town on a Saturday night when the rest of the crew did.

That suited Watrous. He could get along with Colter who was always as smooth as a piece of expensive silk. The Mason boys and Lannigen were run of the mill cowhands, but not Toy Severe. Watrous had never been able to put his finger on the reason for his feeling, but whenever he looked directly into the man's opaque eyes, he felt as if a snake were crawling up his leg. No one else affected him that way, not even Jim Dunn.

"I'll be glad to give you a hand when you make the arrest," Severe said, very casually as if it would be no trouble.

For just a moment Watrous hesitated, glancing at Colter who was eying him with sardonic pleasure. He knew that once he had taken the bull by the horns, he didn't dare let go. For the first time since he started wearing a star, he had the respect of the men at the bar, all except Doc Finley anyhow, but if he started taking suggestions, he'd be right back where he started from.

"No," Watrous said in a positive tone. "Three of us will be enough."

Severe shrugged. If he felt any resentment, his weather-puckered little face did not show it. Without another word, he wheeled and walked back to where he had stood. Watrous glanced again at Colter, then moved to the front door, puzzled by this. Colter's face was covered with scabs and purple bruises, he was dirty, and he hadn't shaved for three days or more. That wasn't like him. Another thing struck Watrous as being queer. It should have been Colter, not Severe, who had offered his help.

Watrous stopped at the bat wings, looking through the glass door that was closed today to keep the cold out. He kept turning this question over in his mind and getting no answer. If Colter had been fired along with his crew, why were they still hanging around Cairo? There would be no other job for them around here, particularly at this time of year. By the time Hofferd and Royal returned, Hofferd with a Winchester, Royal with a double-barreled shotgun, Watrous still had no answer to his question about Colter.

Doc Finley came to stand beside Watrous who was watching the corner around which Jim Dunn should come any minute. It was snowing much harder now so it was hard to see even as far as the end of the block.

"Hank," Finley asked, "are you going through with this?"

"Yes."

"Three men have died from lead poisoning this week," Finley said. "If you arrest Jim, it's a fair guess there'll be another one or two. Maybe you."

Watrous didn't answer. This thought had been in his mind, of course. He was no hero. He had told himself that over and over, and this last week he had even admitted that he wasn't a good sheriff, but he had sensed a change in attitude when he'd kicked young Logan and sent him sprawling and then told everyone he would stand for no more guff.

The feeling that it aroused in him was definitely exhilarating. He liked it. So he ignored Finley, and a moment later the doctor stomped back to the bar. He poured himself a drink and gulped it. Then he pounded the bar, making the glasses rattle.

"By God, Raff, did you ever see as many fools filling men's pants as you do right here?" Finley demanded.

Rafferty, his eyes on Colter and Severe at the other end of the bar, said, "No, Doc, I never did, but the trouble is they ain't all fools."

Chapter XIX

Jim and Ann left Box D early that Saturday morning in a buggy, a buffalo robe over their laps, a fur around Ann's neck. Her cheeks bright with the cold, she pressed hard against his side, and now and then he felt her shiver. They rode in silence as they crossed the valley and wound up the steep mesa hill, Ann not once glancing at Jim.

He wondered why she wanted to stay here. She was not a ranch woman and she never would be. Apparently she was absolutely satisfied to have Maggie serve her meals in the dining room, sleep in her bedroom, and spend most of her waking hours in her private parlor.

A strange woman, he thought, and certainly a fascinating one. He did not understand her at all, but it seemed to him she would be happier in a city with its comforts and luxuries close at hand than on a ranch. But in his own mind at least Jim was now sure of one thing. She had spoken the truth when she said she knew nothing about Sherman Dunn's murder, if it was that, and she was finished with Bud Colter.

They were wheeling across Ruby Mesa before she spoke. "Who do you think fired the shot at us last night, Colter?"

"Sure."

"So I did make a mistake bringing him here," she said with more bitterness than Jim had ever heard in her voice. "I didn't believe he killed Sherm, but now I'm beginning to think he did. I know they quarreled just before Sherm's death. Colter took advantage of every opportunity he had to be with me and Sherm was jealous of him. He thought there had been something between us, but there wasn't, Jim. There never had been. I've only lied to you about one thing. That was my age. I suppose it was the most stupid thing I've done."

"Yes," he agreed. "It was."

She looked at him for the first time since he had helped her into the buggy. She said slowly, "I've tried to make you understand how I feel, but I know I haven't. It was just that I had so many years of insecurity. I did leave home when I was fourteen. I've had to make my own living since then. I got so tired of traveling all the time, usually by stagecoach over all kinds of roads and through every kind of weather. The places where I worked were even worse, with stale tobacco smoke and drunks pawing at me, and lots of times I'd dance the length of the bar and slip on beer someone had spilled and fall down. They'd laugh like fools and it seemed there was always a man who would get up beside me and try to help me up and then want to dance with me."

She stared straight ahead at the road that was whitening with the snow. She went on, "They'd throw money at me. Silver and once in awhile a gold piece. I'd have to get down on my knees and pick the money up. Do you know what it is, Jim, to pick up money that men throw at you and have to hear the things they say and all the time you have to keep smiling at them? No, you couldn't know. You could never understand what it does to your pride when you're trying to hold your self-respect. I wanted to be respectable, but I never was to the women of Cairo. Some drummer came through town who recognized me and then everyone knew."

"I'm sorry," Jim said. "You know what I think of Cairo and what they think of me, but it's different with a woman. I don't know why you want to stay here."

"That's the part I'm trying to explain," she said. "I loved Sherm because he took me away from everything I was telling you about. I loved him because he fixed up my parlor just the way I wanted it. I told you he gave me the first peace and security I ever knew. He was gruff sometimes, and the things that people said about him hurt him more than he let on, but he was always kind to me, and I tell you I loved him and I know he loved me. After they brought him in that day, I had a feeling I was living in a paradise that wouldn't last."

He was silent then, feeling sympathy for her, but

knowing there was nothing he could do. He couldn't let her stay. He didn't want to hurt her, but somehow he had to tell her. He was still puzzling over it when they came down off Ruby Mesa.

"It would have been different if that shot had never been fired last night," she said with regret. "You would have kissed me and you would have forgotten your scruples. We could be happy, Jim. It wouldn't make any difference if I am twelve years older than you are. Or that I loved your father. I could love you more, Jim. You're younger, and in many, many ways you're a better man than he was."

"No," he said.

She sighed. "All right, Jim. Marry your Ginny. I hope you'll be happy." She glanced at him and he saw she was close to crying. But she went on in a low tone, "Kind of funny, in a way. Sherm was in the winter of his life and you're in the spring of yours. I'm in between. I'm October. Late October."

She tipped her head back and looked up at the snowflakes that were so thick the visibility was cut down, and they were on the bridge before Jim realized it. "Sherm always said you could expect a storm in October. Well, we're having it. I won't go back to the Box D, Jim. I'll leave from here. Maggie can pack up my things and send them to me. I'll let you know."

They turned into Main Street, a sudden and

poignant relief in Jim. He had not expected it to be this easy. She had tried and failed; she had done everything she could to hold to the island of security that was the Box D, and she had failed. But she had proven to him she was all that Maggie thought she was. When he pulled up in front of the bank, he said simply, "Thanks, Ann."

She hid her feelings behind the brightness of her smile. "Think kindly of me, Jim. That's all I'll expect from you."

He got down and held his hand up to her, saying, "I can't help doing that."

"Dunn."

Hank Watrous appeared on the sidewalk, a cocked gun in his hand, the barrel lined on Jim's stomach. He must have been waiting for some time because he was so white he looked like a snow man. He was jittery enough to be dangerous, Jim saw, so he stood there, motionless, while Watrous moved closer until he was only two paces away.

"I'm arresting you for the murder of Frank Castleman," Watrous said. "Don't resist arrest or you'll be shot. Hofferd is in the street and Royal is on the other side of you. Both have you covered, and I have given them orders to shoot if you make a wrong move. If any shots are fired, Mrs. Dunn will be in danger."

For a moment Jim was too shocked to say anything. He didn't know that Castleman was dead.

For him to be accused of the murder was too ridiculous to merit discussion. He said, "I didn't kill Castleman."

"We didn't expect you to admit it," Watrous said, "but you're under arrest just the same. Take off your gun belt and lay it on the buggy seat, then step away from it."

"Go inside, Ann," Jim said.

"Don't make trouble, Jim," she cried. "Hofferd and Royal are here."

He hesitated, struggling with an impulse to make a fight out of it, but it would be suicide. He said, "All right, Ann. Go inside." He waited until she was in the bank, then he laid his gun belt on the buggy seat. "Hofferd, will you see that my team is taken care of?"

"Sure," Hofferd said. "We can't leave 'em out here in the street until you're tried and hung."

Watrous tipped his head to indicate that Jim was to move away from the buggy, and when Jim had, Watrous stepped forward and picked up the gun belt. Hofferd got into the seat and drove the team away. Watrous said, "You know where the courthouse is. Start out."

They went down the street, Watrous and Royal close behind. It was like a bad dream to Jim, as weird and impossible as any dream he'd ever had. They went into the courthouse and down the hall and through an anteroom into the jail. When the heavily barred door swung open, Jim asked,

"Mind telling me what the evidence is you've got against me?"

"Castleman was shot," Watrous said. "Murdered from close up. You're the only enemy he had. We know you beat hell out of him the first morning you were in town."

"When was he killed?"

"Dunno for sure. I suppose it was some time last night."

"I was home all night," Jim said. "Mrs. Dunn can swear to that. So can Alec and Sugar."

Watrous looked at Royal significantly. "I expect Mrs. Dunn would swear to that, all right. Well, I'll tell you something, Dunn. Her word ain't worth a damn. Not after Bud Colter said what he did in Rafferty's place the other night."

"You fool," Jim flung at him. "You chowder-headed, locoed, filthy-minded son of a . . ."

"Calling me names ain't gonna do you no good." Watrous slammed the cell door shut and locked it. "Now cool off. If you don't hang, I miss my guess."

Watrous walked out and went on down the hall, Royal following. Suddenly Watrous realized he was sweating, and when he stepped out of the court-house into the cold air, he shivered. He looked at Royal and said, "Well, we done our duty. Let's go get a drink."

"Yeah, sure." Royal sighed with relief. "For a minute I sure thought he was going for his gun."

"Hell, we'd have cut him down," Watrous said. "He knew it, too."

He was bragging, and he knew that Royal would recognize it for what it was, but he told himself he had reason to brag. He had arrested a hardcase without a shot being fired or any difficulty at all, and he had him in jail. No sheriff could have done any more. Now maybe some of the loud mouths would shut up. He strutted a little when he went into the saloon and crossed to the bar.

"Whiskey," Watrous said to Rafferty. "For me and my deputies. Shep'll be along purty soon. We're celebrating. Jim Dunn's in jail."

Rafferty's fat face turned cherry red. He set out a bottle and three glasses, and he said in a low tone, "By God, Watrous, I hope all three of you choke on it."

Watrous stared at him, astounded at Rafferty's tone, although he knew the saloon man was a friend of Dunn's. He did not realize Judge Riddle was there until he felt something hard poke him in the back. He wheeled, hand going to the butt of his gun, but he didn't draw when he saw that it was Riddle who had prodded him with his cane.

"What the hell are you . . ." Watrous began.

"Shut up." Riddle's face was as white as his hair or mustache. "Listen, Watrous. You're a little man. When you pinned on that star, I thought you might grow into at least a pint-sized man, but you didn't. You're still a teaspoon man. Now you're going to listen because I'm a big man. I'll tell you why I'm big. It's because I'm standing beside such a damned little one."

Anger flared in Watrous. He had only done his duty. No one, Judge Riddle or anyone, had the slightest right to talk to him that way. He opened his mouth, but the quick, bright flame of resistance died when he looked at Royal, then at Bloch and Flanders and the rest. They were all meek enough now.

Almost every man in Cairo was here. A few farmers who had braved the storm and had come to town as usual on Saturday morning. At the far end of the bar the old Box D crew was watching, Bud Colter grinning derisively and Toy Severe's weasel-like face showing his pleasure.

"All right, I'm a little man, Judge," Watrous said, "but I done what I thought was my duty. If you've got anything to say, let's have it."

"You're going to get it." Riddle leaned forward, his weight on his cane, his built-up shoe flaring outward. "You didn't do your duty, Watrous. You arrested a man because you don't like him, and you don't like him because of what his dad's bank did to you. Moreover, you've come in for a lot of deserved criticism because we've had three murders in a week, but you sit on your butt yelling that you don't know who did them. So, to drown out the criticism, and to satisfy lunkheads like Bill Royal and Shep Hofferd, you had to do something. Arresting Jim Dunn seemed the easiest thing to do."

"Judge, you're out of line," Royal said hotly.

Riddle wheeled on the storekeeper and rammed the end of his cane into Royal's belly. "No I'm not. I'm going to give you a lecture on money matters you'd better listen to. You know we're having hard times. You also know that the Cairo bank is the only one around here that hasn't gone broke. You cuss Sherm Dunn. Some of you, Watrous for instance, lost your farms. You never thought about Sherm's side of it, that he was doing the best he could and in his opinion, it was better to have a solvent bank in a community than carry men who had failed at farming."

Watrous said nothing. Riddle was talking about him and there was no defense he could make. He had blamed the bank and Sherman Dunn because that was one way he could keep from blaming himself. Now, looking at Riddle's angry face, he felt like running. Riddle might just as well have added that he had failed as sheriff, too.

"The point right now is that practically every man in town and a lot of the farmers around town are in debt to the bank." Riddle pointed his cane at Royal. "You'd be out of business today if the bank decided to take your store. Shep." He looked around until he located Hofferd who had just come in. "You borrowed nine hundred dollars on a note six months ago. It's due now. You ready to meet it?"

"Hell no," Hofferd said indignantly. "You know how it's been. I got loaded up on horses I couldn't sell, prices going down like they are . . ."

"All right," Riddle said testily. "That's the way it is with everybody. What you're overlooking is that the bank is the heart of a community. Suppose it's robbed? Or has a run? Or just closes its doors? We're all broke. But to you the bank is some kind of monster and the men who run it are greedy, money-sucking bastards."

Riddle slammed his cane down across the bar. "You damned fools! I asked Jim and Mrs. Dunn to come to town today to talk to me and Doc and Fred Hines about the bank's policy. I was going to recommend that we rock along in the hopes times will get better. That's a risk, of course. To be safe, I suppose we should force the collection of every note and mortgage the bank holds. Legally, of course, we can do that. I'm not sure what Jim and Mrs. Dunn were going to say, but I know what Jim's thinking right now."

The cane rammed at Watrous again, and it seemed to him that the Judge's mustache bristled more than ever, that his white plume of hair was waving back and forth in indignation. Riddle said, "You let Jim go. Apologize to him. Get down on your knees if you have to, then send him down to the bank and hope to hell he's big enough to forgive a bunch of two-bit bastards who arrested him."

Watrous wanted to stand firm, to say again he had done his duty, but he looked at Riddle and licked his lips and knew that he could not. When he walked out of the saloon, there was no sound at all except the labored breathing of the men behind him. Riddle waited a moment; he stared at Royal and then Hofferd and shook his head in disgust and walked out.

At the far end of the bar Toy Severe asked, "What'll Jim Dunn do?"

Colter laughter softly, for now the current was running his way, the first time in days. He said, "What any man would do. It's gonna make Dunn a mighty popular corpse."

"That's the way I figure it," Severe said. "Get your horses and start out of town, then circle back. Wait till you hear a shot. I'll take Dunn when he leaves the bank."

"Ain't the snow gonna be too deep to get over the divide?" Lannigen asked.

"No," Colter said. "It's one place they won't look this time of the year. Besides, the snow will cover our tracks the way its coming down now."

He went out with Ash Mason and Lannigen, throwing a silver dollar on the bar as he passed Rafferty, but Toy Severe remained where he was, frowning thoughtfully as his right hand gently eased his gun up and down in the holster.

Chapter XX

Orie Mann occupied the cell across the corridor from Jim's. He peered through the bars, asking, "Who are you?"

Jim didn't answer. It was warm in the jail. He took off his Stetson and sheepskin and tossed them into the corner and lay down on the cot. Mann asked, "What'd you do?" When Jim still didn't answer, Mann gave up in disgust and returned to his cot.

Jim lay with his fingers interlaced behind his head, his eyes on the ceiling. The first flare of hot fury had died in him. He knew he would never be convicted of murdering Frank Castleman because there was no evidence against him, but there was a chance a lynch mob would brush Watrous aside and take Jim out and hang him. Evidence and logic meant nothing to men, once mob contagion seized them.

Right now all he could do was lie here and wait. In a way he was glad this had happened. It simply confirmed what he had thought. They were little men, Watrous and Hofferd and Royal and the rest, all but Riddle and Doc Finley, men without either guts or brains.

Now he thought he understood the town. Like

letting down the bars on Saturday when the farmers came to shop during the day and the cowboys to raise hell at night. He had supposed that Cairo somehow reflected his father's spirit. And Riddle's. But he'd been wrong. He knew that from the way the women had treated Ann. And the way the townsmen felt about Sherman Dunn.

Cairo was the people who lived here. On six days of the week they were themselves. On Saturday they did everything, perhaps anything, they could for a quick profit. Not today, for a storm like this would keep the Saturday crowd down. But on most Saturdays that's the way it was. Watrous, no law man at all, was exactly what the town and county deserved.

What kind of a man had his father been? There was another question he had pondered ever since he'd been back. Now he thought he had the answer. But it wasn't a real answer. Just an explanation. Sherman Dunn had been one kind of man to some people, and quite a different one to others. Certainly Watrous and Royal had seen him one way, Ann another.

But Sherman Dunn was dead. The important thing was that he had got along with people who hated him. Perhaps he had lived apart from them. He had been big enough to create his own world, and the others, lacking his size and power, had been forced to live along the fringe of the world he had created. Perhaps that was why they had hated him.

Watrous came into the jail, red-faced and apologetic. He unlocked Jim's cell, and when Jim stepped out, he handed his gun belt to him. "Reckon I made a mistake, Dunn," Watrous said. "We all make mistakes. I hope you won't hold this one against me." He swallowed. "Judge Riddle wants you to come to the bank."

Jim buckled his gun belt around him, then put on his sheepskin and Stetson. He said, "I feel sorry for you, Watrous," and went out.

He strode along the sidewalk, the wind pressing against him and plastering his back with snow. He went into the bank, shut the door, stomped snow from his boots, and hanging his sheepskins and Stetson on the wall, started toward the back room.

Young Buckley, the teller, said, "Go right in, Mr. Dunn. They're expecting you."

In spite of himself, Jim thought, he'd be following in his father's footsteps. No doubt Sherman Dunn had come into the bank many times just as Jim had now, and Buckley, or whoever had been here before him, had said, "Go right in, Mr. Dunn. They're expecting you."

"Thanks, Buck," Jim said, and pushing the gate open at the end of the counter, walked on past Buckley to the door of the back room that served as Hines' private office as well as a conference room.

Jim found them all there: Riddle sitting with his chair against the opposite wall, Doc Finley

225

and Fred Hines on the right, and Ann beside the door. Hines rose and shook hands with Jim, a slender man with the pale face of one who worked inside and the tight-lipped mouth that Jim considered typical of bankers.

"Glad to see you, Jim," Hines said. "Heard a lot about you since you got back."

"I wouldn't be surprised," Jim said, and nodded at Finley. "Judge, there's no use in taking a lot of time for this . . ."

"I don't propose to take a lot of time," Riddle said. "I can only apologize for what happened this morning and say I'm sorry. Now we're going ahead with this meeting and we'll hold it in a businesslike manner. Sit down, Jim."

Ann reached up and pulled him down beside her. She whispered, "I'm not leaving the country, Jim. I'm going to stay at the hotel for a while. The Judge suggested it."

It would have been far better if she'd get out as she'd said she would, but when Jim looked at her, she was sitting with her hands folded sedately on her lap, her eyes on Riddle as if anything and everything he said was gospel. Jim understood them, and he had to struggle to hold back a smile. Ann knew what she wanted; she would use any weapon she possessed to obtain it. As for Riddle, he must have decided she was not the devil in disguise after all. But what would Ginny think? Jim did smile then, and he had to tip his head and stare at the floor, hoping the Judge would not ask him what was funny.

"You all know why we're having this meeting," Riddle was saying. "Our job is to give Fred some general instructions to go by. However, I want to mention one element that none of us can be sure about, and that is the general financial condition of the country, say six months from now. Personally, I think it will improve. What's your opinion, Fred?"

"I think it will," Hines answered, "but there are a few cases that we'll have to deal with separately, regardless of our general policy. If a man has been behind for two years or more, and has paid nothing on account in spite of promises, I think we must take steps."

"And get cussed for it," Jim said.

"We can expect that," Riddle said. "Now then. I hope we can reach a unanimous agreement this morning. Whatever we decide may be a mistake, but it will be better if we agree to the mistake than to have one of us say six months from now that he voted against what was done."

Riddle looked around the room, then asked, "Shall we vote?" No one answered, so he said, "All right, we'll proceed. Doc?"

"Leave it in Fred's hands," Finley said quickly.

"Fred?"

Hines shifted his weight uneasily. He said, "This puts me in a difficult position, Judge. I would prefer to go over the list of names with the amount that is owed . . ."

"No," Riddle said. "That's the bank's business. One of us is bound to let something slip he shouldn't. The proposition is simply this. We're voting to leave this up to your judgment, keeping in mind at all times that the basic point involved is to keep the bank solvent, but extending credit wherever it is possible."

"All right then," Hines said. "I so vote."

"Mrs. Dunn?"

Ann hesitated, waiting for every man's gaze to be focused on her, then, with her eyes pinned on Riddle's face, she said in her clear, sweet voice, "I know that Sherm trusted Mr. Hines' judgment implicitly. I vote to leave it in his hands."

"Jim?"

He reached for tobacco and paper. "You fixed it so I'd have my tail in a crack, didn't you, Judge?"

"Why, no, I . . ."

"Judge, I hope you'll be my father-in-law some-day." Jim sealed the cigarette and put it into his mouth. "I've got a lot of respect for your judgment. Fred here may know banking from A to Z. If Ann says Dad trusted him, that's good enough for me."

He dug a match out of his vest pocket and lighted his cigarette. "But Dad's the one who got the blame. Now I'm getting it. All right, if these men figure I'm like that, I will be. I vote to cut every one of 'em off at the neck and not take any chances on the bank going broke."

There was a long moment of silence. All of them stared at Jim as if expecting this and yet not quite believing it, then Ann put a hand on his arm. She said, "I know how you feel. I've suffered at the hands of these people, too. So did Sherm. But I think you're wrong, Jim, looking at it in the long run."

"Let me ask you one question," Riddle said. "Do you feel this way because you were arrested just now?"

"Not entirely. I guess it's mostly the town. I was Sherm Dunn's son, so they were down on me. I used to be a young hellion, so I must be the same thing now."

"Not everybody thinks that," Riddle said.

"All of them except you people and Rafferty," Jim said. "I say the rest are little, no-good, stinking people who blame everybody but themselves for their trouble. When I need help, do I get it? No. I'm going after Colter. I've got to, but I'll do it alone. Why? Because there's not a man in this town with guts enough to back me up."

None of them said anything for a minute. Then Hines said, "I'll go, Jim."

"I would if I could," Ann said. "I'm to blame for this. I guess you do have a right to hate me."

"No," he said. "You were wrong about Colter. We'll let it go at that. And I didn't mean you, Fred. You belong here in the bank. If you were out sashaying through the snow with me you'd be a liability. I'm talking about the men who arrested me and the rest of them who stood around and let it happen." He rose. "What about it, Judge?"

"We'll postpone making a decision for a few days," Riddle said heavily. "The meeting's adjourned except for one thing, Jim. You've got to make your own tracks, not follow in Sherm's, or get sore because the wind drifted some snow into the tracks he left."

"I aim to make my own," Jim said. "Let them all know I'm the one who threw the monkey wrench into your plans."

He opened the door and walked out. Before he reached the front of the bank, Doc Finley caught up with him. "I'd like to talk to you a minute, Jim."

"A little preaching maybe," Jim said. "About snow in Dad's tracks?"

"No preaching," Finley said. "Just some of my practical experiences. You say these people are little. They are. They know it, too. You're big because Sherm was big. You've come back to the Box D. That's something no other young man in this country could do. You didn't grow up to size because of anything you did."

Jim reached for his Stetson and put it on. "Throw away your black bag and get a pulpit, Doc."

"No, no." For once Finley's face did not have

the rose-checked appearance of an adolescent. He was worried and he showed it. "Because I'm a doctor, Jim, I know these people better than anyone else. I've seen them in all kinds of tragedies. Accidents. Sickness. Hard times like we're having now. I've got better than ten thousand dollars on my books I'll never collect, but I know that if I ever get into real trouble that they can do something about, I'll find out they're pretty big.

"Sometimes, Jim, you'll find bigness where you don't expect it. Honesty, too. Responsibility. All the virtues." Finley smiled briefly. "Take Watrous. I suppose you figure Watrous for the smallest man in the county, but he'll surprise you. His baby's sick. He should have called me three or four days ago, but he didn't because he owed me a bill and he didn't want it to get any bigger." Finley nodded pleasantly. "Give it a little more thought, Jim."

The doctor left the bank, and Jim, standing at the window, soon lost him in the swirling snow. Well, he thought sourly, he'd had his sermon. To hell with all of them. He pulled on his sheepskin. All but Ann. He hoped she got what she wanted.

He went outside, pulling the collar up around his neck. He'd get the team out of the livery stable and head for home. There were three inches or more of snow on the ground now. The higher slopes would have more, but he'd have his look just the same. At Monument Rock. There was another cabin near the head of Rabbit Creek. He'd see about it . . .

"Dunn," a man called from the street. "Make your play."

Toy Severe's voice! Jim dived headlong toward the horse trough ahead of him as a gun roared, its ribbon of flame lashing out into the gloomy light of the storm, the bullet splintering the top of the trough an inch above Jim's head.

CHAPTER XXI

For an instant Jim lay belly flat in the snow, an instant in which he had to decide what to do. He pulled his gun from holster, knowing he had no margin of time for wrong guessing. Severe would be moving toward the trough. What would he expect Jim to do? Certainly not lie here on his belly and be shot in the back when Severe rounded the end of the trough. The logical guess was for Jim to wriggle forward to the far end, hoping to use the trough for cover until he located Severe.

So, because it seemed the logical thing, Jim didn't do it. Instead, he put his left hand against the snow, drew his knees under him, and drove as nearly straight up as he could, like a jack-in-the-box escaping from its prison.

232

A man was running along the walk on the opposite side of the street under the wooden awnings where the snow had not piled up enough to smother the pound of his boots. He shouted, "Severe, Severe!"

Jim was aware of this other man as he came to his feet. Severe must have been, too, for he started to turn just as Jim appeared above the trough, then swung back. He fired, the red tongue of powder flame licking out into the falling snow. Either he was diverted by the man across the street, possibly rattled a little, or he was surprised by Jim's action. In any case, his shot was a clean miss.

Like many professional gunmen, Severe depended on his quick reflexes, on sheer speed rather than accuracy, hoping to get in two shots to his enemy's one, and therefore have twice the chance of scoring a hit. But today his advantage was not enough. Jim fired before Severe could squeeze the trigger again. He hit Severe in the left shoulder and knocked him back and half around as if he had been jerked by an invisible rope so that when he did pull the trigger, his bullet was wide. Jim, firing again, hit him in the chest. Severe went down, his arms flung out, his slack fingers letting go of the gun butt, and blood began drooling from the corners of his mouth.

Watrous crossed from the opposite side of the street. Only then did Jim realize who it was that had called to Severe, and by so doing, had possibly been a factor in making the gunman miss his first shot. For a moment they faced each other, the snow swirling between them, then Jim said, "I suppose you want me for this."

"Don't be a fool," Watrous said in a tight voice. "I'm glad you're alive."

Other men moved into the street and converged on Jim and Watrous: Royal, Hofferd, Herman Bloch, Flanders, Rafferty still wearing his white apron, and others. Before they got there, Jim said, "I don't savvy, Watrous. You'd rather see me dead than alive."

Watrous shook his head. "I ain't satisfied you didn't kill Monte Smith and Frank Castleman. If I get any proof on either one, I'll jail you again." He motioned toward Severe's body. "This was different. If you hadn't dived for the horse trough, he'd have killed you. I know I ain't a hero, but that don't mean I cotton to the idea of a gunslick shooting another man down in the street, even a man I don't like."

The others were there now, staring at Severe, their shoulders hunched forward, coat collars turned up against the cold. They looked at Jim, then at Watrous, and finally Rafferty said, "That was damned good shooting, Jim."

"Anybody see it but me?" Watrous asked. When no one said anything, he went on, "Severe tried to make it a sure thing. He was waiting when Dunn came out of the bank. He had his hand on his gun, figuring that Dunn would recognize his voice and make his play. Instead Dunn got foxy and dived behind the horse trough."

For some reason their faces looked friendlier to Jim than on any previous occasion. Of the men standing here, only Rafferty might be called his friend. Then Hofferd said, "That Severe was a snake if I ever saw one." Jim knew then. As with Watrous, they disliked Severe more than they did him.

Watrous saw Finley running toward them with his black bag in his hand, and called, "We'll lug him over to your place, Doc. It's Severe. Dunn shot him dead." Without a word Finley wheeled and started back. Watrous said, "Shep, get hold of his shoulders. We'll tote him over there."

"Wonder where Colter is," Rafferty said. "He was in the saloon, but he pulled out along with Ash Mason and Lannigen. Severe stayed at the bar. Struck me as being queer then."

Instinctively Jim's hand dropped to his gun, his gaze lifting to the opposite side of the street. He should have known that Colter would be in town if Severe was. Probably Colter, knowing Severe was faster with a gun than he was, had put the gunman up to this. But Colter and his men would still be around. Or would they, if they had been sure Severe would survive the fight he was going to provoke?

Jim could think of only one thing that would

take them out of town. Revenge was always a driving force in a man like Colter. If he had finally given up hope of owning the Box D by marrying Ann, he still might try to burn the buildings as a parting gesture before he left the country.

Only Rafferty stood in the street. The rest were drifting back to their places of business except Hofferd who was helping Watrous carry Severe's body to Finley's place. Jim ran after them, calling, "Hofferd, have you seen Colter and the rest of his bunch?"

Hofferd looked back over his shoulder. "Yeah. They came in a while ago and got their horses. Said they was leaving the country."

"Did you see them leave?"

"I didn't follow 'em," Hofferd answered, "but they rode down the street."

"Which way?"

"East."

That proved nothing, of course. They might have swung south later. Jim thought of Maggie out there on the Box D, and Alec Torrin and Sugar Sanders. They wouldn't even see Colter and his men ride up, snowing the way it was now. Colter could kill the three of them before they knew he was there.

"Watrous," Jim shouted. They had reached the front of Finley's office and again they stopped and looked back. "I'm guessing that Colter headed for the Box D to burn it out. You coming with me?"

He fully expected the sheriff to turn him down. He wasn't sure the man would be any help anyhow, but he was remembering what Finley had said in the bank, about finding bigness and courage where you didn't expect it. Actually Watrous had shown surprising courage in calling to Severe. He must have known that Severe might have turned and shot him, and if so, he had figured the risk and taken it.

Now, at this distance with the snow falling between them, he could not see the expression on Watrous' face, but there was a moment of hesitation, and then Watrous said reluctantly, "Yeah, I'll go."

"I'll get my team," Jim said.

As he turned toward the stable, he heard a sharp crack from the bank, like a shot from a small pistol. Ann was still in there. Maybe Colter hadn't left town. Ann would be a hard woman for him to give up. Jim started toward the bank on the run, but before he reached the corner of the building, he heard the roar of a .45.

Jim's first thought was that Colter was trying to make Ann leave town with him, then the possibility that someone was holding up the bank occurred to him. It might not be Colter at all. Either way, there had to be horses and none were racked along the street. He looked back and saw that Watrous and Hofferd had dropped Severe's body and were coming on the run.

"Take the front," Jim yelled, and sprinted along the side of the building.

Whoever it was must have come in through the back. He cleared the corner of the building, his gun palmed. A man was mounted, holding the reins of two other horses. A second man with a sack in his hand ran out of the back door. Both were wearing slickers, and both had bandannas over their faces. Jim had no way of recognizing either.

The mounted man gave out a high yell and threw a shot at Jim that was wide by a foot or more, then his horse began to buck. The second man never tried for his horse. Jim fired at him and apparently missed, for the fellow whirled and bolted back through the door. The mounted man was having trouble. He got off a second shot that was wild. No one could have shot straight from that hurricane deck. He lost the reins of the other two horses, and for a moment there was a wild melee of bucking horses with so much snow kicked up into the swirling flakes that Jim couldn't see anything clearly.

He held his fire, momentarily undecided what to do. Since there were three saddled horses out here, two men must be inside. Watrous and Hofferd had them bottled up from the front, but there was no telling how they would handle the situation.

The duel between horse and rider lasted only a moment, for now the man came flying through space to crash against the back wall of the bank. All three horses went down the alley on the run. When Jim reached the thrown rider, he was flat on his back, knocked cold. Jim yanked the bandanna off his face. Ash Mason! Colter, then, must be inside.

Jim wheeled and lunged through the back door, fully aware that he was taking a long chance. The man who had come out and dived back inside might be waiting for him. But the hall was empty except for Watrous who was coming from the other end.

"We got Crip Lannigen," Watrous yelled.

"Mason's in the alley, knocked cold," Jim yelled, and for a moment he was completely puzzled by the disappearance of the third man who must be Colter.

The stairs! In this wild, frenzied moment he had completely forgotten about the stairs. He jerked the hall door open and took the stairs three at a time. Before he was halfway up he was suddenly aware of a woman's shrill, sustained scream. It seemed to him she had been screaming all the time, but he had just then become conscious of it.

There were two sets of offices over the bank, Judge Riddle's in front, and Reno Flanders', an insurance and real estate agent, in the back. When Jim reached the upstairs hall, a girl who worked for Flanders was standing in front of the open door that led into one of his office rooms. Her mouth was wide open, but no sound was coming out. She stood as if frozen, right arm held straight out from her body, forefinger extended.

When she saw Jim, she screamed, "A man! Had a gun. Went through the window."

Jim wasted no time on the girl who, except for being thoroughly scared, wasn't hurt. He leaped over a chair that Colter had apparently knocked down, and rushed on to the window that was still open. If Colter had dropped to the ground from there, he might have been stopped by a broken leg or sprained ankle, but the instant Jim looked out of the window he saw what had happened. The jewelry store next door to the bank was a one-story building. Colter had dropped to the roof below the window, slid off to the ground, and disappeared. Marks in the snow below plainly showed what had happened.

Jim holstered his gun, crawled through the window and let go. When he hit the jewelry store roof, he lost his footing and sat down hard. There was nothing to hold to or check his descent, and he went on off the roof like a floundering toboggan to slam into the bank wall, bounce back against the jewelry store, and from there fell to the ground. For a moment he lay in the snow, his mind working, but for some strange reason, his body refused to obey his mental orders.

Colter would try for a horse. He had to, but the horses in the alley were gone. Colter would guess that if he hadn't run back to look, and he probably hadn't because he'd remember that Jim had been in the alley.

Slowly Jim rolled over on his stomach, forced himself to his hands and knees and then on up to his feet. He leaned against the bank wall, felt for his gun, and found that it was still in his holster. He took one step away from the wall and looked at the ground. This was the way he had come when he'd gone around the bank to the alley, and although there wasn't much snow here in the narrow passageway between the two buildings, there was enough to show fresh tracks leading to the street.

"Dunn." Jim lifted his head to see Watrous looking down at him, his head poked through the window. "Where'd he go?"

Jim motioned toward the street. "He's out there somewhere. You get Mason?"

"Hofferd's taking care of him. What'll I do?"

"Come down the front stairs."

Jim's legs were operating now. He ran to the street, remembering there were no horses racked at the hitch poles except a few in front of Rafferty's that some farmers had ridden to town, but they were slow, plow horses, and would be worse than nothing for Colter. There was only one place he could go, Hofferd's livery stable.

Watrous appeared. "The bastard shot Mrs. Dunn. Tore a hunk of meat off her right arm, but she's gonna be all right. Where do you figure he went?"

Jim jerked his head toward the stable. "Getting himself a horse. Come on."

"Wait a minute." Watrous knelt in the snow and pointed to a red spot. "He's bleeding. The Judge figured she plugged him. In the left hand, he thought, but hell, that little pop gun of hers wouldn't hurt him much."

Jim started toward the livery stable on the run, Watrous panting and trying to talk as he ran beside Jim. They went past the Mercantile, Rafferty's place, and several smaller buildings before they reached the stable. Jim stopped and put an arm in front of Watrous.

"Hold up," Jim said. "Mighty dark in there. If Colter's in one of those stalls, he'd pick us both off if we went in after him."

"Well, what'll we do?" Watrous asked.

It was the second time in five minutes that Watrous had asked for instructions. Jim said, "We'll figure a little bit. Has Hofferd got any fast horses?"

"Yeah, a black gelding he calls Midnight. Faster'n your Sundown. If Colter gets on him, he'll get clean away."

"Where does Hofferd keep him?"

"Last stall on the right side." Watrous took a long breath. "We can't just stand here, Dunn. He's got some time bulge on us anyhow. If he slaps a saddle on that black . . ."

"Which won't be easy with his hand boogered up." Suddenly Jim was aware that armed men were converging on them: Rafferty, Bloch, Royal and others. Cairo had finally stirred into action. "If we let this bunch move in, and Colter's hiding in one of those stalls, he'll kill or wound half a dozen men."

"But damn it, we can't just stand here and let him ride out through the back door." Watrous wiped the snow off his face and stared at Jim, suddenly frantic. "I'm going in, Dunn."

Chapter XXII

Jim grabbed the sheriff's arm, thinking of what Finley had said, that sometimes you find courage where you least expect it. But this might not be courage. Watrous intended to do what he said, but to Jim there was a difference between an act done in a moment of excitement and that which a man would do after considering the factors involved.

"Stay here," Jim said. "Make the rest of 'em stay with you."

Jim wasn't sure Watrous would obey, but he didn't wait to see. He ran along the side of the building to the alley, wondering if Colter would really take time to saddle a horse. That undoubtedly had been his reason for coming here, but would he, not knowing how much time he had? He certainly realized that within a matter of minutes the town would be aroused and after him.

Colter was hurt, he was alone and on the run, and panicky. More than that, he was basically a coward. He had proved it at the bunkhouse when he'd fought with Jim. He could have pulled his gun and hadn't. He'd proved it when he'd shot at the window last night, and again just a few minutes ago when he'd come through the back door of the bank building. All of his size and inordinate vanity, his tough talk and black clothes, which were an affectation with him, did not change his insides.

So it was no surprise to Jim when he reached the alley to find fresh tracks leading toward the rear of the Mercantile, with here and there a drop of blood in the snow. From the back door of the stable Jim called, "Come on, Watrous, he's still running."

Somewhere the man intended to hole up and hide until evening, if he was thinking that far ahead. Maybe he couldn't even extend his thoughts past the point of hiding. He could have ducked into one of the narrow openings between two of the small buildings: the drugstore, Hattie Jones' millinery shop, or some of the others. If he had, Jim was risking his life every time he went by one of those long, narrow passageways, but he didn't think Colter would do that. Like a wounded animal, he'd try to find a warm, dark place in which to hide, probably Bill Royal's big storeroom with its innumerable barrels and boxes and sacks.

Jim was so certain Colter was headed there that he was almost past the loading platform behind Rafferty's saloon before he noticed that the fresh tracks he had been following were no longer in front of him. He wheeled and ran back. Watrous and the rest were streaming down the alley from the stable. Jim wished the others would stay out of it. The more of them there were, the bigger the chance of some getting hurt. The kind of help they would give in a pinch was questionable, anyhow.

Jim waited behind the drugstore until they came up. He said, "Colter's given us the dodge. He's hiding around here somewhere. Chances are a few of us will get killed before we root him out."

He watched them back off, all but Rafferty and Watrous. Hofferd said, "I'll go back and look in the stable. He might be up in the mow."

"You do that," Jim said. "Royal, go take a look in your storeroom. Rest of you scatter out and look between buildings. He might have gone in some of the back doors."

They left, reluctant to obey Jim's orders, but

refusing to let their fears completely possess them. Watrous remained, watching Jim eject the empty shells from his gun and reload. He stood there until Jim finished checking the action of his Colt and had replaced it in his holster, then he said, "All right, Dunn. Where is he?"

"In Rafferty's storeroom," Jim answered. "Can't be any other way. He's winded and he's been shot and he's scared, so he finally holed up. I'm going in after him, Watrous. You're staying outside."

Watrous made no objection, but he frowned. "Lot of barrels in there," he said dubiously. "Be hard to find him. Why don't we wait till he gets sick enough to come out?"

Jim shook his head. "I can't prove it, but I know he killed Dad. Lennie, too. I've waited too long now. I've got it figured. He'll get back in the corner as far as he can. There's just one little window, so with the door shut, it'll be dark inside."

Watrous nodded agreement. "That window's dirty and covered with cobwebs. On a day like this there won't hardly be any light come through it."

Jim rubbed his right hand against his pants leg. The snow had slackened off, but there was more wind and he was chilled. He closed and opened his hand, looking down at it and thinking of Lennie and how he'd died without a chance, then he climbed up on the loading platform.

The door into the storeroom was closed. The tracks did not lead inside. Instead it appeared that Colter had walked across the platform close to the wall. For a horrible moment Jim thought he had fallen into Colter's trap, that he had been wasting time thinking he had the man cornered while actually Colter had jumped off the platform and turned toward the street, following the narrow opening between the store and the saloon. But when Jim reached the edge of the platform, he saw that there were no tracks on the ground.

Jim glanced at Watrous who was standing beside the platform. "Tricky," Jim said, and motioned for Watrous to climb up. He pointed to the tracks. "Thought we'd think he was a bird."

Watrous frowned. "The tracks don't go no place. He couldn't be inside. He got to here, but he didn't go back."

"That's what he wanted us to think," Jim said, "but he should have known we'd look for tracks on the ground. I guess when you get to the end of your twine, you take the first thing you think of."

Jim walked to the door. Watrous followed, still puzzling over what seemed a mystery to him. "How'd he get inside? If he'd jumped off and gone around the platform, we'd see his tracks."

"He backed up in these tracks," Jim said. "Had to. Only way to explain it." He drew his gun. "Soon as I go in, slam the door behind me.

He'll think it's the wind. Keep the door shut till I holler. And don't stand in front of it."

Jim threw the door open and dived in. Colter fired instantly from the far side of the room, the bullet slapping into the wall just above Jim who lay belly flat on the floor. Watrous had shut the door and now it was very dark. Jim began worming his way toward the inside corner, wedging his body in between the wall and the heavy barrels.

"Stay where you are," Colter screamed. "Don't come any closer."

Jim said nothing. He crouched in the corner, wondering how he would get between the wall and the end barrel which was full and too heavy to move. If he got any closer to Colter, he'd have to go over the barrel. He hesitated, not sure whether there was enough light in the big room for Colter to make out his movement or not.

Now, this close to the finish, Jim couldn't remain motionless. He had one advantage. Colter did not know his exact location. If he moved fast, he'd be over the barrel and on the floor again before Colter realized what he was doing. He got slowly to his feet, then dived over the barrel and hit the floor hard, making a great racket and drawing a shot. Again he remained motionless, finding himself now between the wall and a row of empty barrels. He knocked one over purposely and Colter fired immediately.

Jumpy, Jim thought, jumpy enough to do anything.

Jim moved forward, and suddenly he was aware of a new sound along the platform side of the room. Colter was working toward the back door. The strain was too much. He was going to make a run for it, not knowing Watrous was outside. If he went through the door in a rush, he might get out before Jim could shoot, and then it would be up to Watrous who was still, as far as Jim was concerned, an uncertain quantity.

A minute dragged by, then two, and again Jim heard the dragging sound of Colter pulling himself toward the door. Once more Jim tipped a barrel over and Colter fired at the sound. He was close to the door now. Jim waited for what might have been another minute. His time sense was completely out of focus, but he wanted to wait just long enough for Colter to reach the door.

"Watrous," Jim yelled. "Open the door."

He moved as he shouted. Colter fired at the sound of his voice, the bullet ripping through an empty barrel and striking the wall within inches of Jim's head. The door swung open and in the sudden burst of light, Jim saw Colter's big body dive forward. Jim fired and rose and fired again, but Colter was still on his feet, his legs straining desperately to get him to the edge of the platform so he could be out of the range of Jim's gun.

Jim plunged toward the door, wondering

where Watrous was, then he heard his gun as Colter crumpled and spilled over the edge of the platform. Jim had to slow up and work his way through the maze of barrels and boxes. By the time he got through the door and reached the edge of the platform, Colter was dead, his body sprawled on the ground, the snowflakes settling on his black clothes and pearl buttons and the shiny, silver belt buckle, and blood was bubbling in a scarlet froth between his lips. Somewhere he had rid himself of the bandanna and slicker.

"He was hard to put down," Watrous said. "You hit him twice and I got him once." Watrous looked up the alley and then glanced the other way. "Look at 'em come. Funny thing how you get all kinds of help when you don't need it."

"It's always that way," Jim said, "but you're the gent I don't savvy. I figured you'd be hiding under a bed somewhere."

Watrous' face was gray and tight when he looked at Jim. "I dunno, Dunn. Sometimes you do things when you have to that you don't think you can."

"Well, you don't need me now," Jim said, and turning, walked through Rafferty's storeroom and on into the empty saloon.

For a long time he stood at the bar. He poured himself a drink and felt the jolt of it hit his stomach, then he stood staring at the empty glass. It was over! The knowledge brought its easing of tension. Tomorrow Luke Dilly would be here and they could go to work. They had a ranch to run.

He rubbed a hand over his face. But it wasn't all over. There was more to this than the Box D. He was remembering things people had said since he'd got back. Doc Finley: "You're big because Sherm was big. You didn't grow up to size because of anything you did." Judge Riddle: "What we do with the bank is going to decide the life and happiness of almost every man in the valley." And Rafferty: "You'll go easy on 'em because you're a hell of a decent man."

But most of all it was Ann who more than anyone else had reason to hate the people of Cairo, who could be expected to use the bank to destroy those who had done all they could to drive her from the country. She'd said: "I can forgive them because I'm bigger than they are." That was true, but what did it make Jim Dunn?

He took another drink. It did no good. He threw a coin on the bar and turned to the door. Of all people, she had taught him a lesson in forgiveness; Ann Dunn whom he had hated for three years. When the six months was up, the bank would probably go to her and the ranch to him. It was only right that the bank should be run the way she wanted it. So his mind was made up when Rafferty came in through the street door.

"Where's Ann?" Jim asked.

"In bed in a hotel room. . . ."

Jim didn't wait to hear the rest. He went out into the storm, and leaning against the wind, battled his way to the hotel. He pulled the door open and stepped inside and shut the door, then beat the snow from his clothes.

"Well, you did it," Riddle said, "with a little help from Watrous. We owe you quite a bit."

"Yeah," Bill Royal echoed, "we owe you quite a bit."

The Judge was standing by the stove. There were several other men with him including Fred Hines and Reno Flanders. Because it was foremost in his mind, Jim said, "Judge, about that business we were discussing in the bank. I'll go along with Ann and the rest of you."

Hines nodded, Riddle smiled, and the rest looked puzzled. Riddle said, "I figured you would, when things ironed out."

Jim felt better. It had been a hard thing to say and he was glad it was done. He asked, "What happened in the bank?"

"We were standing there talking," Hines said, "and Buckley was working on the books at the desk when Colter and Lannigen came in. They had guns on us before we knew what was going on. They made Buckley fill the sacks, but they weren't watching Mrs. Dunn very close. She got her gun out and shot Colter and he shot her. She started to fall and the Judge tried to hold her, but he was off balance and he fell, too."

"My damned knee," Riddle said apologetically. "It was Ann that saved the bank. Wonderful woman."

"Colter lit out for the back door," Hines went on. "Lannigen was behind him. The Judge reached out with his cane and hooked Lannigen's ankle and brought him down. That gave me and Buckley a chance to jump him."

"Lannigen and Mason are in jail," Riddle said. "They told us that Colter shot Monte Smith and Severe killed Castleman."

Flanders said, "That's what we figured. Hell, we knew it wasn't you, Dunn." Bill Royal nodded as if he, too, had known it all the time.

Jim looked at Royal and he turned his head to stare at the snow-dappled window, suddenly red in the face. It was just as Watrous had said when the shooting was over. You get all kinds of help when you don't need it. An hour or so ago Flanders and Royal would have helped hang him, but now it was different. He would never like them, Jim thought, but he'd have to get along with them.

Jim asked, "How's Ann?"

"In bed and she'll be there awhile," Riddle said, "but she'll be all right. She's got to be."

"Jim."

He whirled to see Ginny coming down the stairs. He went to her, his arms outstretched, and she ran to him, and for this moment there was no one in the world but them. She clung to him with desperate urgency as if she would never let anything take him from her again, then she drew her lips back and said softly, "I didn't really know why you wanted me to wait, about Colter and all. You've got every right to scold me, but please don't. I've been upstairs with her. She said people learned to like her once they knew her. That's what was wrong. None of us ever took the trouble to know her."

"You will," Jim said. "About that six months. Well, there's no need to wait now."

"Jim, Jim," she breathed, "that's what I wanted to hear."

Over by the stove Judge Riddle stroked his mustache, he patted at his white plume of hair, and then he asked, "Gentlemen, has there ever been a double wedding in this town?"